b o o k s   t o   r e a d . . .

TIMAS PUBLISHING GROUP

Istanbul 2009

www.timas.com.tr
www.timaspublishing.com

THE MISSING ROSE
Serdar Özkan

TIMAS PUBLISHING GROUP | 2099
Literature-Fiction | 3

EDITOR-IN-CHIEF
Emine Eroğlu

EDITORS
Zeynep Özbek
Cüneyt Dalgakıran

COVER DESIGN
Ravza Kızıltuğ

COVER PAINTING
Pity by William Blake

FIRST PRINTING
July 2009, Istanbul

THIRD PRINTING
October 2009, Istanbul

ISBN
978-605-114-025-4 (Hardcover)

PRINTED AND BOUND BY
Entegre Matbaacılık
Sanayi Cad. No: 17
Çobançeşme-Yenibosna-Istanbul
Tel: (0212) 451 70 70

TIMAS PUBLISHING GROUP
Alayköşkü Caddesi, No:11, Cağaloğlu, Istanbul
Tel: +90 (212) 511 24 24 Fax: +90 (212) 512 40 00
P.O. Box: 50 Sirkeci / Istanbul

www.timas.com.tr
www.timaspublishing.com
timas@timas.com.tr

Publishing Certificate No: 12364

Translated from Turkish by Angela Roome in cooperation with the author.

The Missing Rose

Serdar Özkan

* Translated by Angela Roome

TİMAŞ

To S. Catalanta

and

to all real roses...

O Rose, thou art sick:
The invisible worm
That flies in the night,
In the howling storm,
Has found out thy bed of crimson joy;
And his dark secret love
Does thy life destroy.

William Blake

Thou shouldst enter a garden
Thou shouldst journey through it
Thou shouldst smell a fresh rose
A rose that never fades...

Yunus Emre

Prologue

Ephesus! City of duality. Home to both the Temple of Artemis and the holy House of Mother Mary. The city which embodies both the ego and the soul. The epitome of both vanity and humility, the personification of enslavement and freedom. Ephesus! The city in which opposites intertwine. The city that is as human as every living soul.

One October evening, two people were sitting by the side of the Meles Stream near that city—the ancient city of Ephesus. The sun was about to hide itself behind Mount Bulbul, dyed crimson by its rays. Those who understood the language of the skies had brought them the glad tidings of the approaching rain.

"Saint Paul is preaching to the people about Mother Mary," the young woman said. "Can you hear the crowd yelling, protesting and cursing him in anger? Thousands are rebelling against the new religion which forbids them to worship their own goddess. Listen to them stamping their feet and shouting, 'We don't want Mary! We worship Artemis!'"

"Artemis?" the young man asked. "The goddess? The Roman Diana?"

"Don't mind her," the young woman said. "She's nothing but an illusion, shaped and worshipped by others."

"You seem to know a lot about her."

"I know her like I know myself."

"Well then, won't you tell me something about her?"

"She is the goddess of the hunt," she began. "A true huntress who uses her arrow to offer a sudden, sweet death to her enemy. Free-spirited yet enslaved, dependent yet proud. Supported by an olive tree, her mother Leto gave birth to her and ..."

After taking a deep breath, she added, "And to her twin ..."

Part One

1

Two are one…

Only one. Yes, of course! Of course, there is only one bottle.

No, that's not true... I see two bottles.

But maybe, maybe I'm seeing double, maybe there's still a chance there's only one bottle…

No, I can't be that drunk, I can't be seeing double. There must really be two bottles.

Yes, okay, there are two bottles. But why are there two? Why two?

Oh, god, they look exactly the same. Their size, shape, color are exactly the same, even their goddamned production date is the same! Yes, they are… They are twin bottles!

But how? How could one bottle suddenly be two bottles? How could this happen?

And why?

It's not fair...

In one of Rio de Janeiro's most voluminous and beautiful homes, set on a hill overlooking the bay, the same scene that had been played almost every night for the last month was now being played over again. Buried among the cushions of the black sofa in the narrowest corner of the huge living room, Diana, with her wine-bottles, lay trying to understand how her life had so suddenly turned upside down.

Tonight, like every other night, the things she'd suppressed during the day now weighed on her like a ton of bricks. Her body was as numb as it had been every other night; her chestnut hair was as tousled and her green eyes were as bloodshot. Those bloodshot eyes looked from the two bottles on the coffee-table to her mother's photograph on the mantelpiece and then back again.

The only apparent difference from the other nights was the fire she'd lit especially to burn the two letters. The shadows of the flames flickering on Diana's face on this warm May night fanned the fire within her.

She drank down the last sip from the wine-glass in her hand and dropped it on the floor. Before gathering her strength to reach for the second bottle, for a moment, she turned her eyes towards the bottle she'd just finished.

"You know," she said to the bottle, "you're just like me; even though you're finished, you're still standing up shamelessly." She smiled wryly. "After all, we're goddesses, aren't we? What can knock us down?"

Then she turned to the second bottle. "As for you, you mother-thief!" she said. "Mom says that you and I are twins. But for me, you're nothing, nothing but an illusion."

Diana raised herself up from the cushions of the sofa and leaned towards the coffee table, but instead of reaching for the bottle, she picked up her mother's letter which lay next to it. That letter which, in a matter of minutes, had made one bottle become two bottles.

Her mother had given this letter to her a month ago, the day before she passed away. She'd told Diana to read it only after she died, saying, "This is my last wish, darling. I want you to promise me you'll carry it out."

Diana had asked what it was her mother wanted her to do, but her mother had not answered her question. Instead, she'd fixed her deep blue eyes on Diana, patiently waiting for her daughter's promise. It had been as if those eyes would never yield; so in the end, no longer able to withstand her mother's pleading gaze, Diana had given her word.

On hearing her promise, her mother's eyes had regained their old sparkle, and her pale face had come alive for a moment. She'd placed Diana's hand within her own and said, "I knew I could depend on you, darling. Please look after her, look after her very well. She is unique."

Bending towards her mother, Diana had asked, "She? Who is she? Who are you talking about, Mom?" But her question had remained unanswered until after her mother's final departure from her the following day.

When Diana had opened and read the letter, she felt as if the ground had slipped from beneath her feet. Sinking slowly to her knees, she'd read the letter over and over again, feeling all her remaining strength drain out of her.

Since then, little had changed.

Before placing her mother's letter into the fire, Diana read it one last time:

April 1

My Dearest Diana,

I hope you're well, my darling. You must keep well. You mustn't ever believe you've lost me. I know it's not easy. But I beg you to try…

Please don't forget to let me know how you're doing once in a while. Scribble something to me in your diary, talk to my photograph, write stories to me…

As soon as the time of your graduation is fixed, let me know. And please don't give up your evening walks. You're going to your classes, aren't you? Any news of your job applications? Above all, please tell me as soon as you start writing beautiful stories again like you used to. Who knows, perhaps very soon you'll give me the joyful news that you've finally decided to become a writer. What is it really, darling, that's preventing you from pursuing your greatest dream? But, as always, it's for you to choose. All I want is your happiness.

I say 'your happiness,' Diana, but what I have to tell you in this letter may cause you some despair. Please know that this isn't my intention. But I'm afraid I have no other choice. Forgive me...

I really wish I could discuss with you face-to-face what I'm about to tell you. But, as you can see from my scrawled handwriting, I no longer have the strength to confront you with this news nor to give you all the details. My only hope now is that God will help me get to the end of this letter.

I don't quite know where to begin...

And even if I did, I couldn't. Because in order to begin, I have to go back twenty-four years, to the day when you were one year old, the day on which you last saw your father.

Diana, my darling... The truth is, your father never died. But he left us. And he left us taking your twin sister Maria with him...

So that you wouldn't feel the pain I felt and wouldn't grow up feeling like a child abandoned by her father, for all these years I've let you believe that he was dead. I even put up that gravestone which, while we were living in Sao Paulo, you visited every month thinking it was your father's. But, in any case, he was as good as dead to both of us.

When we moved to Rio de Janeiro, it was as if we'd left the past behind us. I never told anyone here that your father was alive nor mentioned anything about Maria. I knew that your father who'd separated us from Maria would never let us see her again. He must have told her a story similar to the one I told you.

You must be asking, quite rightly, why I'm telling you all this now. Let me explain...

About a month and a half ago, your father was informed of my illness by a mutual friend and must have wanted to clear himself of blame by giving Maria my address. But I know he didn't tell her about you or about my illness.

From then on, I received a letter from Maria once a week—four letters in all. But never with any return address. She wrote that she was looking forward to coming to see me soon. A week ago, however, I got this note from her:

"Mom, I can't bear being without you any longer. If I can't be reunited with you, there's no point in living. Oh, Mom… I want to kill myself… Maria, March 23."

As far as I could tell from her letters, your sister seemed so full of life that I still can't believe she'd write such a thing. And since she has my address, I can't understand why she didn't come to see me.

As if that note weren't enough, yesterday your father phoned. It was the first time he'd called in twenty-four years. As soon as I heard his voice, I knew he was calling about Maria. Indeed his first words were, "Do you know where Maria is?" He went on to say that about two weeks earlier, Maria had gone missing, leaving a farewell letter behind—you'll find it attached to this letter; your father faxed it after our conversation. He told me they'd searched everywhere for Maria and consulted all her friends, but had found no clue as to where she might be.

Oh Diana, in the little time I have left, there's nothing I can do now. I'm so afraid… You are my only hope. So I have no choice but to ask you to please find your twin and take care of her.

I am so sorry to be adding more pain to your grief and burdening you with such a responsibility. But I feel even more sorry to be leaving behind another daughter who spent her whole life hoping to meet her mother.

Knowing how much you love me, I have no doubt that you'll do everything you can to fulfill this last wish of mine. But I know finding Maria won't be easy. There's absolutely no clue as to where she may be. Our only hope is the fact that in her letters she has left a door half-open for me into the extraordinary world she's created for herself. Hers is a deep, secret world, one to be found in fairytales; yet at the same time, it is so real. I'm sure she hasn't shared it even with her father or her closest friends; that's why I think we have a better chance of finding her than anyone else has.

What I'd like you to do is to step into Maria's world and follow the footprints she's left behind. After all, who could do this better than her identical twin?

All the information we have are the three names Maria wrote in her letters, "Zeynep", "Socrates" and the name of a palace. These names alone may not be enough to trace her. But unfortunately, that's all we have.

Maria's letters are in the antique chest. You'll find the key to it in my jewelry box.

Diana, I hope you and Maria will soon be united, just like you once were within me.

And when that happens, please write to me…

Diana, my darling, this is not a time to say goodbye. No time is. Please never forget, I am always with you. And I love you very much.

Your mother

2

Diana unfolded the farewell letter Maria had written to her father. It was now time for it to turn to smoke.

March 17

Dear Dad,

I have to leave home today.

You must be wondering why.

Yesterday, after so many years, I read St. Exupéry's Little Prince again. The book seems to have changed completely! The only thing that hasn't changed is that the rose is still my favorite character. And the fox, of course; because it is he who teaches the little prince how to become responsible for his rose.

I think at last I'm also beginning to understand what "being responsible for a rose" means. And that's the reason why I'm leaving.

At the end of the book, St. Exupéry urges us to ask ourselves, "Has the sheep eaten the rose, yes or no?" He says the answer to this question changes everything.

So I'm asking myself a similar question:

"Have Others stolen my rose, yes or no?"

St. Exupéry was right; the answer to this does change everything. But I know that no grownup will ever understand why.

I'm leaving because my answer to this question is "yes."

I'm leaving to reclaim my rose...

Maria

Diana turned to the bottles once again. "Tell me, bottles!" she said. "Tell me what on earth all this means... Doesn't it all seem quite mad? To take off after reading a book... To go missing on account of a rose? What's all this about? Reclaiming one's rose, being responsible for a rose...

"No, no, I'm not interested in knowing what the rose in *The Little Prince* stands for, nor in what it means to that girl. I really couldn't care less! All I want to know is, why it's *me* who has to pay because some girl I've never even seen left home and then wanted to kill herself?"

She fell silent, angry with herself for appealing for help to the bottles she'd despised such a short while before. But who else was there? Who else except these bottles would listen to her?

"How true Mom's words are," Diana murmured. "She said Maria was unique... Of course, of course she is unique. The way she stole my mother from me is truly unique."

After a moment of silence, Diana crumpled Maria's letter in her hand and threw it into the fire. "Forgive me, Mom," she whispered, watching with an expressionless face as the ball of paper slowly turned to ashes.

3

Startled, Diana awoke to the sound of the doorbell which, despite its melodious chime, cut like a knife through her aching head.

"Senhora Lopez! Senhora Lopez! Please answer the door!"

Receiving no reply, she remembered that it was Senhora Lopez's day off. Holding onto the sofa, she dragged herself up. Hardly able to stand, she made her way to the door.

On looking at the security camera, she could see that the unwelcome caller was Gabriel, the courier who regularly delivered flowers or all kinds of beribboned packages to her.

When she opened the door, she found Gabriel standing with yet another beribboned package, its top reaching almost to his chin. His brown face, brown overalls and brown hat were a perfect match for the color of the package.

"Good day, Miss," Gabriel said. "I have yet another gift addressed to Rio's most beautiful girl. Would you know if she happens to live here or not?"

"Isn't it a bit early to be delivering parcels, Gabriel?"

"Well, this must be the right address then. But maybe the wrong time?"

"What time is it?"

"It's already noon."

"Is it really that late?"

Diana took the package and signed her name in the delivery book in a scrawl that resembled any signature but her own. And before Gabriel could say his usual, "Take care till the next time your admirers bring us together," Diana shut the door.

Receiving prettily gift-wrapped packages always used to make her day. This time, however, she wasn't the least bit interested in knowing what was inside the package, nor who'd sent it. She left it there on the floor and headed back to the sofa.

As she walked past the mirror in the hall, she noticed wine stains on her shirt. She suddenly remembered her mother; a happening which she'd become accustomed to these days. Somehow, a small or seemingly unrelated thing was enough to take Diana back to her life with her mother. A color, a smell, a word, and now this stained shirt... The memory of the day she'd bought this shirt and the conversation she'd had with her mother afterwards came to life as if it were only yesterday...

For Diana, it had been just one of those shopping days. At the boutique, she'd first debated whether she needed a new shirt or not, telling herself she'd done enough shopping that day already, but finally she'd ended up buying yet another yellow shirt.

When she showed it to her mother, Diana didn't bother to conceal from her the R$ 2200 price tag.

After glancing at the price, her mother asked, "Darling, did you read about the Paris auction in yesterday's paper?"

"No, Mom, why?"

"A vest belonging to Descartes was auctioned for R$ 250,000."

"Oh, really? I'm glad we weren't there. You wouldn't have bought it and it would have stuck in my mind. Anyway, look, my shirt is much smarter than Descartes' vest, don't you think?"

"All of R$ 250,000, Diana!"

"Oh, all right, I see what you're getting at. You're trying to tell me that R$ 2200 isn't really too much to pay for a shirt like this, aren't you, Momma dear?"

Diana knew perfectly well that wasn't what her mother had in mind, but she wanted to use her charm to pass it off lightly, so she could go and happily hang up her new shirt along with all the others.

"Well, you're right on one point, darling. Your shirt is certainly smarter than Descartes' vest. His vest wasn't made of silk or cashmere, nor was it from Donna Karan or Armani. In fact, it wouldn't cost more than R$ 30 at the mall."

"Still, the auction price makes sense, Mom. I mean, the vest was worn by Descartes!"

"True. Being worn by a person like Descartes certainly increases the worth of a piece of clothing. But can you imagine the reverse?"

"What do you mean?"

"A piece of clothing increasing the worth of a person ..."

Diana hung her head for a moment. She'd realized what her mother, in her own inimitable way, was once again trying to say: "The only thing you need in order to feel special is yourself."

"I know what you mean, Mom, but people always want to see me wearing the best. As soon as they see me, they look me up and down from my shoes to my hair and only then do they say, 'Hi.' If I wear the same clothes two days running, they look at me in horror.

"Do I like being judged by my appearance? Or seeing the insincere respect in people's eyes? Their whispers about my couture collection, my Cartier, my Maserati, my this, my that ... No, Mom, I really don't like it. But you know that it's because of who we are, that everyone, at every moment, expects the best of everything from me."

"And you believe it's your duty to live up to their expectations, darling, is that it?"

"What can I do? We're not living in the jungle."

Smiling playfully, she added, "Admit it, Mom. Diana Oliveira has become a trademark. How can I disappoint my public, those fans of mine who shower me with endless adulation?"

Five months ago, however, from the moment the doctor had uttered those few words, many things in Diana's life had changed.

"We're going to lose your mother," the doctor had said.

4

The kitchen with its medicine cupboard seemed so far away. Everyday the house was becoming larger and larger for Diana; the distance from the living room to the kitchen, from the kitchen to the bedroom and from the bedroom to the bathroom were all getting longer. For a month now, she hadn't gone down to the basement where the swimming pool was located, or climbed to the upper floor with its terrace and art studio, so she had no idea whether the way there had become longer, too. Nor did she have any desire to find out.

When she finally reached the kitchen, she poured herself a glass of water and drank it in one gulp. Then another. And a third, this time with two aspirins dissolved in it.

She journeyed back to the living room. As she headed for the sofa once again, her cell phone rang. It rang a second time, a third, a fourth... After the seventh ring, she decided to answer it.

"Happy birthday! Happy birthday! Happy—" howled a young man's voice.

Diana immediately cut the connection, and threw the phone onto the table.

Was it true?! Was it really her birthday? Did someone have to remind her of that?

In the past, however, she would always count the days till her birthday and make plans for it in advance, preparing a list of people afterwards in the order they'd celebrated her.

The first name on this list had always been her mother's.

This would be the first birthday she would spend without her. The first of all the rest of her birthdays...

Her eyes filled with tears.

She went to the cabinet and searched through several drawers before she finally found her diary. Sitting on the floor, she opened it and began to write.

My Beloved Mother,

You said you were always with me... If you are, then why do I miss you so terribly?

I just learned that today is my birthday...

Oh, Mom... Where are you?

Forgive me, Mom, for not having replied to you sooner. It's just that this is the first time I've opened my diary since you went away…

No, I'm not mad at you because of your confession. Maybe in the beginning, I was a little angry, perhaps a little heart-broken, too, but it didn't last long. I'm sure you had good reasons for keeping the truth from me.

But I'm sorry, Mom; I never searched for Maria. I'll never forgive her for causing you to live your last days in worry and fear. I didn't even read her letters, can you believe it? Maybe she's already been dead a long time… Forgive me…

You know what hurts the most, Mom? Just because I broke my promise to you, I feel like I can't even keep you alive in my heart. Everything always reminds me of you, but this only makes things worse… I feel like I can't remember you in peace… If only she hadn't showed up, things wouldn't be like this.

And I'm not interested in knowing about that man, either. I'm sure you had enough reason to believe that he was as good as dead to both of us.

Anyway… Let me answer your questions, Mom…

Today is the last day of school. I'll still be graduating among the top three of my class. The ceremony is on May 19th at 5 o'clock. You can't imagine how much I wish you could be there…

To be honest, I haven't been taking my evening walks. But don't worry, I'll start again as soon as I feel less tired.

As far as my job applications are concerned... Last week, two of the best law firms in the city both offered me a job. They want an answer by the end of the month, but I haven't decided yet which to accept.

I know, you'd tell me to turn them all down and become a writer, instead. I really wish I could do that, Mom. But you know as well as I do that you're the only one who likes my stories. Others think they are no good.

Anyway, I only dreamed of being a writer because of those wonderful stories you used to tell me. It was your stories that added meaning to my life. But now you're gone. And so are your stories. You can never tell me another story and if I did write a book, you could never read it. You could never say, "Oh, that was splendid, Diana."

That's all my news for now, Mom. I hope, somehow or other, you'll know that I'm doing okay.

Diana's eyes stayed fixed on her diary for a while. She'd written this page feeling for a moment that her mother was expecting some news from her. But that was ridiculous! The dead couldn't read the letters written to them nor could they receive news that their daughters were okay.

She closed her diary and walked to the silver frame her mother had had made specially for her as a birthday present. A month before she'd died, she'd held out this frame which had a black rose motif handcrafted on each of the four sides. "Happy birthday, my darling," she'd said. Diana had immediately realized what her mother hadn't put into words and had refrained from mentioning that there were still two months till her birthday.

She caressed the four black roses ornamenting this most precious remembrance of her mother. Then she read aloud her mother's poem written inside the frame:

No, it's not what you think.
You have not lost me;
I speak to you through everything,
From behind the remembrances…

A tear ran down her cheek. "No, Mom, it's not what *you* think," she whispered. "I have lost you. And you don't speak to me."

5

Diana sat down by the package to open it with the hope that perhaps it had been sent by her mother. She was amazed that not even this gift-wrapped package had reminded her of her birthday.

Inside it were a bottle of champagne, a heart-shaped crystal, a birthday card and a love letter with no name on it. Before she had the chance to get up and throw them into the garbage, the doorbell rang again. It seemed there was to be no peace for her today.

On the viewing-screen, she could see the uninvited guests were her close friends, Isabel and Andrea. Those "close" friends who were only interested in how she did her hair, what she wore, how entertaining or how popular she was.

But Diana also knew that it was through friends like Isabel and Andrea that she felt admired, through them she felt special, and through them she'd become *the* "Diana."

In the face of what she owed them, now that they'd come, she couldn't refrain from opening the door or tell them to come later or shout from behind the door, "I don't want to see anyone!"

So she opened the door.

"Happy birthday to you, happy birthday to you, happy birthday dear goddess, happy birthday to youuu!"

Their display of joy ceased when they took in her disheveled appearance.

"What happened to you, Di?!" Isabel asked.

"How many times do I have to tell you not to mix your drinks, Di?" Andrea said. Then, perhaps thinking that the view from the living room wasn't good enough for her, she caught Isabel's hand and drew her quickly toward the steps up to the terrace, as she started firing questions:

"Aren't we having a birthday party tonight, Di? Why weren't you at school? So what's the plan?"

As soon as they stepped out onto the terrace, Isabel ran her finger along the edge of the teak furniture. "There, Senhora Oliveira! This dust is sufficient proof that although the whole city lies at your feet, you've given up enjoying the view. Isn't that right, Andrea?"

"Indeed!" Andrea said.

"Well, Di," Isabel continued, "you haven't answered Andrea's question. What's the plan for tonight?"

"I don't think I'm going to do anything."

"What?!"

"I never like to disappoint you, you know that, but I went to bed really late last night and my head's splitting, so—"

"But today's your *birthday*, Di!"

"I really don't feel like—"

"What's going on with you, Diana?" Isabel said looking at her sternly. "It was you who used to bring everyone together, now we hardly ever see you. We know, you're going through a tough time, we all understand that. But do you think shutting yourself up in the house will help you get over it? Do you think that's what your mother would have wanted? Pull yourself together. You're a strong girl."

"No."

"No what?"

"I'm weak."

"No, you're not. You can't be. You have a long way to go, goals to achieve, dreams… But if you keep behaving like this, you'll never—"

"What dreams?"

"Well, didn't you dream of becoming a successful lawyer?"

Heaving a sigh, Diana first looked at Isabel and then Andrea. They really had no idea, did they?

"I never dreamed of becoming a lawyer, Isabel."

"What do you mean?"

"I only ever dreamed of being a writer."

"Oh, right, that dream!" Isabel said.

"Oh, come on, Di," Andrea said. "We're not kids anymore. When I was little, I wanted to be a singer. But when I grew up, guess what, I realized I have the voice of a crow!"

Neither the friendly expression on Andrea's face nor her appearance of laughing at herself was enough to mask what she was really trying to say.

"Don't worry, Andrea," Diana said. "I already know that I write like a crow."

"I didn't mean it like that, Di, I just—"

"Well girls, we have no time to argue now," Isabel said. "What about tonight?"

Neither Diana nor Andrea replied.

"Di, we should really get going now, we have to go try on our graduation outfits. But we'll come by this evening to pick you up, let's say at around eight. Be dressed and ready so we don't lose time. We'll take you to Olympia or what about Da Mario? And if you like, to Pulana, okay? A few calls and the old gang will get together. How's that for a plan?"

"I'm in!" cried Andrea.

"Well," Diana said. "Thanks a lot, both of you, for coming… But today, I want to be alone."

6

When Isabel and Andrea had gone, Diana stayed on the terrace for a while longer, thinking how little they knew her. For years they'd been friends, they'd laughed and had fun together, sharing so many good times… So how was it that these two girls didn't know her and what she dreamed of? But then, what did it matter if no one understood a dream she'd decided to let go of?

She thought of the question her mother had asked in her letter. "What is it really, darling, that's preventing you from pursuing your greatest dream?"

Diana knew that if she had a thousand lives to live, in each single one of them she'd still want to be a writer. The only reason she'd chosen law was because of the dreaded scenario she envisaged for herself if she were to become just a mediocre writer…

To begin with, those around her would think she'd wasted her qualifications. In spite of this, however, they'd politely conceal their actual thoughts and tell her what an interesting and exciting profession she'd chosen. But there would always be a hidden disapproval and disdain behind their words and soon she would become the subject of gossip. People would whisper the news about the heiress to an international hotel group and one of the most prestigious hotels in Rio de Janeiro, "the unfortunate Diana Oliveira" who had once been the envy of all the young people in the city, admired by everyone, but who eventually ended up being a writer whose books nobody read. Those who would once have given everything to be in her place would pity her thinking that she'd wasted her life.

Diana had never told anyone that it was only because she didn't want to live this scenario that she'd chosen a career which people around her would approve of. So maybe it was her own fault that her friends didn't know how she really felt. But hadn't she tried to tell them about her dreams and hopes? Of course, she had.

But whenever she'd tried, they'd judged her. It was as if they knew what was best for her and always swamped her with advice on what she should do, how she should think and even how she should feel. They never tried to understand.

How was she to face being left all alone in this world, with no one to understand her?

To still her tired mind, Diana eventually decided to take an evening walk down in the park as she'd always done with her mother.

7

The park wasn't too crowded. Getting as close to the sea as possible, Diana walked along the shore.

How many times in the past had she and her mother walked here together, how many times? What would she not give to be able to have one more stroll here with her mother? Just one more...

Lost in her memories she walked for about a quarter of an hour more. When she reached the marina with its sailing ships, she turned for home.

She usually chose to return home by way of the short cut across the park, mainly because she enjoyed seeing the unusual people along the way. People with hair dyed every color of the rainbow, pierced on the least expected parts of their bodies; people who looked for but couldn't find an empty spacc to be ornamented with yet another tattoo...

As usual, the pathway was crowded with vendors of knick-knacks and kitsch, with tattoo artists, strolling musicians and beggars.

As Diana went past the beggars, she heard a deep voice:

"Hey there, little lady!"

Not sure if she was the one being addressed, she glanced around, but couldn't see anyone else who might answer to this description. Then, she caught sight of an old beggar staring at her. Once more he called, "Hey there, little lady!"

She had often seen this man with curly gray hair at this corner, sitting cross-legged on a piece of straw matting. What made him different from his fellow beggars was that, although his small black eyes were constantly searching the crowd for something, he never harassed the passersby. Another difference was that on the corner of his ragged mat was written: "Fortunes Told- R$ 9."

Diana was surprised; she'd passed by this fortunetelling-beggar perhaps a hundred times before, but never once had he called out to her.

"Were you talking to me?" she asked the beggar pointing to herself.

"You're searching for her?"

"What do you mean?"

"Her!"

"Who's her?"

"If you don't know, how come I should?"

"What?!"

"Her, I'm saying!"

She shook her head. There was no need to go on with this strange and pointless conversation. Perhaps he had been waiting for someone to play a joke on, or perhaps he was simply testing a new way of attracting the attention of a possible customer. Whatever the reason, it was enough to make Diana decide to walk away as quickly as possible.

She wanted to continue on her way as though no words had passed between them, but she paused when the beggar called out to her once again:

"See here, little lady, I'm ready to tell your fortune for nothing. Come, maybe your luck will tell you where she is."

"I don't know what you're talking about and I don't want to know, either."

At that moment, quick as a wink, the beggar tipped something resembling ashes into the glass of water in front of him and began to peer at it intently as the water turned grayish. Then, "Oh, my!" he said. "What do I see, what do I see? She's looking like you. Just like you!"

Diana froze where she stood.

"Who looks like me?" she asked swallowing hard.

"That's better, little lady, come sit now."

Diana did as she was told.

The beggar swirled the water with his forefinger before brushing the tip of it on Diana's face. Without waiting for her reaction, he said, "Whether you are searching for her or no, she's looking like you. Just like you! Same age, same height, same eyebrows, same eyes..."

Diana felt a cold shiver run down her spine. She hardly knew what to do or what to say. But there had to be an explanation to this. There was no such thing as fortunetelling, no such thing as mind-reading. There was no chance that this man could be talking about Maria!

To prove he was just a charlatan, she asked, "So, where is she?"

"Not far away."

"Where exactly?" she asked, raising her voice.

The beggar took her hand and poured a little of the dirty water into her palm. After examining it attentively for a minute, he said, "She comes from far away to near. Soon she goes far away, but she comes back again."

Then, he lifted his head and fixed his gaze on something at the other side of the pathway. Diana turned to see what he was looking at.

About twenty yards ahead, a street artist was watching them. When the artist realized they were looking at him, he quickly turned back to his easel. Diana gestured questioningly at the beggar.

"That girl who's just like you," the beggar said, "she gets to meet that artist some day."

Diana sprang to her feet. It'd been a mistake to sit down there in the first place. It was obvious he was just having a joke at her expense. She should have realized it long ago;

there had been a sly expression of amusement on his wrinkled face from the very beginning.

As Diana hurried away, the beggar called after her, "Read. Open what's written and read."

Open and read! These words sped like a treacherous arrow into Diana's retreating back.

Was this also a coincidence? Could these words be related to Maria's letters which she'd never opened, let alone read? Her head was in a whirl, but this time she went on without a backward glance.

Even though she wanted to get home quickly and leave all this behind her, her steps involuntarily slowed as she was passing the young street artist. As he stood facing his painting, she took a quick look at this unkempt youth, to see if she could make any sense of what the beggar had said.

Probably a few years older than her, the artist was tall, well-built, with tanned skin and untidy brown hair. He was wearing an old maroon T-shirt and a pair of blue jeans, worn into holes at the knees. His sandals were too dusty to guess their color.

Propped against the iron railing that surrounded a nearby palm tree stood his paintings for sale. They were all much the same in theme—sky, sea and a seagull in each. Each had a price tag of R$ 150 hanging on it. Although the quality of paint looked poor, the paintings themselves were inviting.

The artist became aware of Diana's gaze as her eyes wandered from himself to his paintings and back again. He turned his big hazel eyes on her. "How can I help you?"

"Oh, just looking."

"But could you see?"

"Excuse me?"

"Well, did you like the paintings?"

"I like your choice of color tone."

The artist remained silent.

Diana, who'd expected at least a "thank you" for her compliment, said, "So... Bye then."

The artist merely waved and without waiting for Diana to leave, became engrossed in his painting once again.

Diana wasn't going to mind the manners of a street artist. At least not today. But as she walked away with steady steps, she couldn't help thinking how uncouth his behavior had been and how unlikable he was.

8

All that was left of the moth which had been flying around the room was a slight haze of smoke around the lamp and a faint smell of burning. Looking at the wisp of smoke, Diana wondered what had driven the moth to throw herself into the light.

She must have followed an instinctive call to fly away from the dark, Diana thought. The urgency with which she flew must have been a rebellion against the gloom that enveloped her. A rebellion against uncertainty. She'd chosen to melt away in the fire instead of flying a lifetime in perpetual darkness.

Wouldn't opening and reading Maria's letters be the same as the moth throwing herself into the fire? Would it be an escape from the darkness she'd fallen into by ignoring her mother's last wish? And if so, to escape from such darkness, uncertainty and disloyalty, should she face the risk of being extinguished like the moth?

Diana didn't know what to think anymore. She didn't know why she was in the dark, how she'd ended up there, or whose fault it was... Was it her fault for not acting upon her mother's wish? Or her mother's for placing such a heavy burden on her shoulders? Her father's for splitting the family in two? Maybe the blame should be put on Maria since she was the one who'd sent that selfish note to her mother. Or maybe on God who had taken her mother from her. Perhaps everyone was to blame, perhaps no one...

She didn't know the answer, yet she could feel that the reins of her life had long since slipped from her grasp. It was as if events beyond her control were determining her thoughts, feelings and actions; as if decisions about her life were being made somewhere, at some unknown place, and put into effect without her knowledge or consent.

Was it fate?

If it were, were those strange words of the beggar who'd never spoken to her before, also a part of that fate? If she got up now, opened Maria's letters and read them, would it be of her own free will? Or would she simply be obeying another command of fate which was dragging her toward the unknown? Perhaps the two were the same thing. She didn't know.

However, there was one thing she did know: She respected that moth.

Diana suddenly got to her feet. She walked straight to her mother's jewelry box, took out the key to the antique chest and went to the room where it stood. She opened the chest and found Maria's letters wrapped in a piece of cloth. With the bundle in her hands, she returned to the living room.

Sitting on the floor, her back against an armchair, she unwrapped the cloth. Inside it, she found four large and one smaller envelope, all of different colors. In the smaller envelope was Maria's last note to her mother. The larger envelopes had all been numbered in her mother's handwriting in the order she'd received them.

The colors of the envelopes were, in sequence, red, green, white, silver. She noticed that the first three had been posted in Sao Paulo, while the fourth as well as the one in the smaller envelope were postmarked Rio de Janeiro.

So Maria must have come to Rio, thought Diana. She suddenly remembered the old beggar's words. "She comes from far away," he'd said. "She's not far away."

If Maria had come to Rio, then why hadn't she come to see her mother? Could she still be here? Did she live in Sao Paulo?

As Diana battled with such questions, she noticed that the silver envelope—the fourth one—was empty. The question of where the letter it had contained might be just added to her confusion.

In the hope of finding some answers, she read through the letters. Then, she picked up the first one again and began to read it carefully a second time.

Letter No: 1
"Objecting to Others"

February 14

My Beloved Mother,

Outside, lightning is flashing and thunder rolling. I'm reminded of the nights when I would curl up in my bed shaking with fear, longing for the refuge of a mother's chest.

Just when I'm about to be overcome by your absence once again, my father comes into my room to confess that you are alive! Holding out your address to me, he says that I can write to you.

The storm outside suddenly becomes my friend. The lightning bolts become camera flashes photographing my joy. "At last," I say to myself, "At last, I'll be reunited with my mother!"

Yes, Mom, it's unbelievable but true. My quest for you, which began such a long time ago, is about to come to a joyful end. In exactly one month's time, I'll be coming to see you!

The thought of meeting you after so many years fills me with such indescribable happiness. Yet, I feel my happiness is incomplete because you don't really know me.

I have recently begun writing a novel to help me introduce myself to you. The story is based on the things I experienced in my search for you. Oh, Mom, if you only knew what I've lived through in this endless search. I've objected to the Others, crossed an ocean and even spoken with a rose!

I wish I could send you a copy of my novel right away, but it isn't finished yet. However, I'd still like to share my story with you. To give you the feel of it, I've decided to send you a letter once a week, telling you about the different phases of my search.

I call these phases: "Objection", "Path", and "Annihilation". The last phase, "Rebirth," will start as soon as we are reunited.

Let me begin telling my story with the phase of Objection…

I was quite young when I asked myself this question: "Why don't I have a mother?"

But no matter how hard I tried, I could never find the answer.

However, if there was a question, there had to be an answer. Of course, I wasn't old enough then to reason like this; but at the time, I could still hear the voice of my heart.

"Don't ask, 'Why don't I have a mother?'" my heart said. "Ask the right question, ask 'Where is my mother?' Ask this to Someone-who-knows."

Someone-who-knows… Someone who knows… Someone with knowledge… My father!

"Dad, where is my mother?" I asked.

After hesitating for a moment, my father said, "Your mother is with God, my child."

Surely, that had to be the truth. Because God would live in the best place and my mother, too, would be worthy of the best place.

And so, "Where is God?" became my next question. My father looked at me as though I'd asked the oddest question in the world. Then, he answered: "I don't know."

Hoping maybe Others would know where you were, I asked them, "Do you know where my mother is?"

"Your mother doesn't exist," they said.

"What does that mean?" I asked.

"Well, she died, she's not here anymore."

How was this possible? This thing, your dying, your being "not here." How could they suggest your absence when I felt your presence so strongly? Once again my heart spoke to me, "You feel your mother's presence, so she must exist."

I went up to Others and said, "My mother is alive!"

They gave me a different answer: "Your mother is some place far away."

I wasn't convinced by that, either, because I felt that you were very close.

They came up with yet a different answer: "You can only see your mother in the next world."

No! There had to be another answer.

"I'll go and search for God, then," I said to myself and asked Others if they knew where He was. If I could find that out, I'd also find out where you were. But soon, I realized that people's views on God were very confused. Some said, "God doesn't exist"; some, "God is some place far away"; and some, "You can only see God in the next world."

Again, there had to be another answer! But at least these answers showed I was on the right track. The clear similarity between Others' answers to the questions, "Where is God?" and "Where is my mother?" proved that you really were with God. Actually, I've recently come to realize that the phases of my search for you weren't too different from the ones in my search for God. In fact, they were the same.

So Mom… As time went by, seeing that my whole being was preoccupied with you, Others tried to distract me from you. They gave me many toys and playthings. These kept me entertained for a while, but soon I grew tired of them. They offered me new ones; more attractive, more expensive, more exciting toys...

Maybe, I thought, if my toys are constantly renewed, and if I am always given better toys, then I can keep myself entertained for the rest of my life. But, no, that's not what I really want. What I want is my mother!

What toy could make me happy if you were absent? But if you were with me, the lack of what toy could cloud my happiness?

So I was able to escape from the toy-trap, but before long, my search for you was interrupted again. Let me explain, Mom...

As I grew older, Others began to pay more and more attention to me. Sadly, they admired me a lot. I say "sadly" because soon I realized that their admiration and my desire to maintain this admiration were stopping me from pursuing my greatest dream—finding you.

I felt that if I kept asking Others questions about you, they would soon turn away from me. That's why I eventually gave up my search for you and instead let myself enjoy the continuing sunshine of their smiles.

Others kept showering me with their arrows of praise and adoration—deadly arrows as I later realized. "You're special, there's no one like you in the whole world," they would say. As they said things like these, the sweet venom of their arrows flowed into my blood.

I still did, at times, doubt the truth of their words. I often asked myself, "Am I really special?" But since it was Others who'd made me believe this, I could not answer this question without them. It was as if the mirror of my soul was broken and I could only see myself as reflected in their words.

I sought to be in their company all the time; so that whenever I asked, "Am I really special?" I could hear their invariable reply, "Yes, indeed you are. There's no one like you in the whole world!"

I never became tired of asking the same question or hearing the same answer over and over again. Just as salty water increases the thirst of the one who drinks it, their praises only increased my need to hear them.

Worse, in order not to lose the approval of Others, I felt bound to live up to their expectations. Soon, I realized that I was living the life Others had chosen for me, not the one I myself had always dreamed of.

Once more, my heart spoke to me: "You are unhappy, Maria."

It was true. I was so disappointed in myself that I could no longer take any pleasure in the admiration of Others. However, it was my unhappiness that finally gave me back the strength I needed in order to carry on my search for you.

"Where is my mother?" I asked Others loudly.

They replied with the same old answers:

"Your mother doesn't exist." "She is some place far away." "You can only see her in the next world."

"No!" I said. "It's not what you think."

"This is what we heard from the others."

"What if the others are wrong?"

"Look around you, you can't see your mother or God. If you were meant to meet them in this world, surely you'd see them."

"If I'd use only my eyes to see, I'd be lost in your dim world."

"Come on, be sensible, you are a big girl now."

"No, I'm little," I said. "And I will always be!"

However, this objection alone was not enough to take me to you, Mom. I had to find a path. The second phase of my search began when, in a dream, you showed me the path leading to you. You told me where I could find that Someone-who-knows. Much later, in real life, this person would take me by the hand and walk me on the path you'd shown, until you and I'd be reunited in this world.

I hope to tell you all about this dream in my next letter.

With all my love…

Maria

9

Dressed in the green linen suit her mother had always liked to see her wearing, Diana strode across the grass toward her mother's grave. As she came closer, she saw a figure with long chestnut hair standing at the side of her mother's headstone. It was the only headstone under the huge plane tree, so she couldn't have mistaken the grave. It wasn't a special day of any kind, so who could this visitor be so early in the day?

Could it be Maria?!

She hesitated to go any further and stood watching the unexpected visitor for some time.

"Who are you afraid of?" she scolded herself, and started walking again toward the grave. She could feel her heart pounding. A few steps were enough to leave her breathless.

But she didn't stop. Even though she'd almost reached the grave, the visitor would not turn to look.

As she got closer, Diana caught sight of the visitor's face; she was relieved to see that it was only Senhora Alves, her mother's traveling companion. The last time Diana had seen her had been at the funeral. Though Senhora Alves had been one of her mother's closest friends, since she lived in Sao Paulo, they hadn't had the chance to see each other more often.

Diana gently touched her on the shoulder. "I'm happy to see you, Senhora Alves."

"Oh, Diana, how are you?" Senhora Alves asked as she embraced her. "Are you all right, my dear? I phoned you so many times, but could never get hold of you. I left a message with the manager at the hotel. She said you were well, but—"

"I'm so sorry that I couldn't get back to you, Senhora Alves. I'm feeling better now."

She nodded toward the yellow roses Senhora Alves had brought for her mother. "How beautiful they are."

Senhora Alves' eyes showed her agreement.

"Diana, I have an appointment at lunch time, and I'll be going back home this afternoon. But if you'd like to come, I'd be very happy to take you back with me."

"Thank you, Senhora Alves, I appreciate it, but there are things I must do here."

"As you wish, my dear, but don't forget, we're always happy to see you..." After a moment of silence, Senhora Alves took Diana's hand. "Now be honest with me, Diana. Are you okay?"

The expression on Diana's face answered her silently as if to say "How can I be?"

"Diana, I know you don't need to hear this from me, but still, let me say it anyway... Your mother was always proud of you."

"I really wasn't prepared for it, Senhora Alves. Everything happened so fast. Five months ago, everything was fine. Even when she was ill. Mom never acted as though she had only a few months left to live. She never let herself go or lost that twinkle in her eye. She never once asked, 'Why me?'"

Diana's eyes filled with tears.

"But I can't be like her, I can't. Every morning when I wake up, I ask the same question, 'Why her? Why did it have to be my mother?' She wasn't just a mother, she was, she was a light shining on everyone around her."

"She was," Senhora Alves said.

"But I never drew near to her light, I never tried to be illumined by her... And just when things might have changed, she went away."

"Changed?"

Diana nodded.

"For some time now, I'd been feeling that I needed to see life through my mother's eyes. I needed to discover her, be like her. I needed to solve the mystery beyond her gaze, her words, her way of life... She had a hidden treasure inside her, and I could never reach it."

A sudden memory brought a faint smile to Diana's lips. "Sometimes... Sometimes I'd tease her. 'Come on, Mom,' I'd say, 'if you think I have a treasure, too, then give me the key to it.' She would show me her empty hands and say, 'I don't have it. Nobody has it but you.'"

Diana heaved a deep sigh. "I needed that key, Senhora Alves. I needed it. I wanted to be like my mother. I wanted to be worthy of her, at least. Do you know what I feel sometimes? I wish she hadn't let me go my own way or allowed me to make my own mistakes. I wish she hadn't accepted me for what I am. I wish she'd tried to make me more like her, as other mothers do. I wanted to be my mother's daughter, Senhora Alves, I really did."

Senhora Alves hugged Diana as she broke down into tears.

"Oh, Diana, you *are* your mother's daughter. You're so like her. I've never known another girl resemble her mother as much. Never doubt that. Maybe I haven't had the chance to spend much time with you. And it may seem as though I'm just trying to comfort you, but believe me, I know you very well, Diana. I've learned so much about you from your mother, who knew you better than you know yourself."

Diana's sobbing ceased. "What did my mother say about me?" she asked softly.

"Last year, on our journey to Alexandria together, she talked so much about you. She told me how unfulfilled you felt, that you were no longer satisfied with what you had, and that every day you were becoming more and more unhappy."

"Yes," murmured Diana, bowing her head. "That's true, about a year ago, I did start feeling that way. But I thought I'd succeeded in keeping my feelings to myself. I didn't want my mother to be sad, especially since there was no real reason for me to be unhappy. But I guess, as always, she was able to see what was going on inside me. I wonder why she didn't say anything to me? How sad she must have felt..."

"Sad? I don't think that was the case at all," Senhora Alves said. "Her eyes were sparkling when she told me."

"Sparkling?"

"Yes, she seemed to be really happy about it. She even said, 'I can see that my daughter is becoming more and more thirsty for the October Rains.' In fact, she was thinking of inviting you to join us on our next journey."

"October Rains? You mean the journeys you used to take every October? Those mysterious journeys?"

Senhora Alves nodded.

"I was always so intrigued by them," Diana said. "Each time I wanted to go with you, but Mom would never let me. And when you came back, whenever I asked her anything about them, all she would say was, 'We listened and we were renewed.'"

Diana's eyes looked at Senhora Alves pleadingly. "At one time, it wasn't more than just mere curiosity for me, but a few years ago, I started feeling that there was more to those journeys, as if those journeys were the source of my mother's light. I feel I would know my mother better if I knew more about them. And you're the only person I know who can help me with this, Senhora Alves. Please, can't you tell me what you did in Alexandria? Or in Athens, Jerusalem, Fez, Surabaya…"

Senhora Alves wouldn't meet Diana's eyes. She seemed sorry to have led the way to this subject.

"I always admired how wonderfully your mother expressed herself, Diana. She put it in the most beautiful way: we listened and we were renewed."

Diana knew it was useless to persist. "I see… Can I ask you another question then?"

"I hope it's not as difficult as the last one," Senhora Alves said, smiling.

"Where is my mother, Senhora Alves? Where is she? I want to know what happened to her. And I'm sure you have a better answer to this question than I do."

After a moment of silence, "Do you remember, Diana," Senhora Alves said, "at the time when I first met your mother, you were asking her the same question over and over again. You were asking where your father was. And your dear mother always gave you the same reply, 'Your father is with God, my child.'"

As soon as Diana heard this reply, she realized that the question she had just asked Senhora Alves was the exact same question Maria had been asking all those years. She wondered why Senhora Alves had answered her question in this way. Since Diana wasn't sure whether or not Senhora Alves knew the truth about her father, she refrained from mentioning Maria to her.

"People may comfort a child who has lost her mother by saying, 'She's with God.' But I'm not a child, Senhora Alves, you can tell me the truth. Please. My mother doesn't exist anymore, does she?"

"What's said to comfort a child isn't always wrong, Diana. Wherever your mother was before she died, that's where she is now. With God."

Diana lowered her gaze.

Senhora Alves touched Diana gently on the shoulder. "Let me leave you to have some time alone with your mother, my dear. But remember, we always have a place for you at home."

Diana hugged her. "Thank you, Senhora Alves. I'll come to visit you as soon as I can. Have a safe trip home."

10

When Senhora Alves was out of earshot, Diana sat down at the foot of the grave. She put her hands on her chest and prayed silently for a while. Even though she didn't believe her mother could hear her, she still spoke to her.

"Mom, did you hear what Senhora Alves said? She said I resembled you more than any other girl resembles her mother. She's such a sweet person. But I suppose there are some things she just doesn't know...

"I wanted to tell you that last night I glanced through Maria's letters, but then I put them away again. Even though it may be too late, I did think of doing what I'd promised you. But I couldn't, Mom. Don't ask me why, I just couldn't.

"I wonder about one thing, though. I wonder what you thought when you read Maria's letters. We both thought the same thing, didn't we? That Maria's mentally ill? I know you told me she was unique, but you said it so that I wouldn't hold back from looking for her, didn't you?

"I'd really like to know what you actually meant by the word 'unique.' As far as I know, this word means 'one and only.' It means there's nothing like it in the whole world. But you didn't use it in that sense, right, Mom? You didn't feel that Maria is more worthy to be your daughter than I am, did you?

"That couldn't be true anyway, Maria's insane. Didn't you read her third letter? How she heard the rose breathing, the breeze blowing through her room, the light illuminating everywhere... And what about the conversation she had with the rose?! If those aren't symptoms of psychosis, what are they? They are nothing but hallucinations. Trust me, Mom, I studied enough Psychology to know that.

"In any case, the things she says in her first letter, the things she claims she realized as a child, are in themselves enough for us to decide she isn't normal. Can a child of that age have such a perception of life?

"And what about the dream she describes in her second letter? Supposedly, in her dream you tell her to go to some garden, meet with some person, and talk with some rose. And many years later, off she goes and does just what you told her to. Finds the person you spoke of, and what's more, learns from her how to talk with roses! Could all these be for real?

"Anyway, don't worry about Maria, Mom. Maybe life is easier if you're not quite right in the head. Don't worry about me, either. Perhaps I'm suffering because I'm still sane, perhaps I can't be convinced that I haven't lost you and perhaps I can't help thinking that you no longer exist... But in spite of all this, I will not go crazy, Mom. I will not try to escape from reality and I will not create a fantasy world for myself. Because I am a big girl and I always will be!"

Diana got to her feet. "And one day," she added. "I am going to conquer all this pain and succeed in being your daughter."

11

After returning from the cemetery, Diana spent most of the day sleeping. Although she had many things to do—bank payments to make, graduation preparations, e-mails to answer, etc.—she kept on putting it all off for another day.

She just didn't feel like doing anything, but to sit doing nothing only increased the emptiness inside her. Eventually, she decided to go for a walk along the shore.

The park was more crowded than it had been the previous day, but she found a secluded corner where she could sit and watch the children throwing bread to the seagulls. After a short walk, she sat again, this time to watch the sun sink slowly into the ocean.

On her way home, she again took the shortcut; she wanted to go past the beggar in the hope that he might give her a clue as to what he'd meant by his words the previous day.

As she approached the spot where the beggar was sitting, she saw he was examining his surroundings in the same way. Pausing in front of him, she stared him directly in the eye. To her surprise, he took no notice of her. Instead, he went on turning his head this way and that, watching the other passersby as if the girl who now stood in front of him wasn't the same girl he'd spoken to a day earlier.

"Hi, won't you tell my fortune today?"

The beggar appeared to have no idea what she was talking about.

"Do I know you?"

"Don't you remember? It's me."

"I know it's you. But who are you?"

Diana, now quite certain he was just fooling with her, turned on her heel and marched away.

A few paces further on, she noticed the artist, busy painting. He was wearing the same old shirt and blue jeans. She couldn't see much that was different in the painting he was working on, apart from a greater mass of foam from the breaking wave.

"You look better today," the artist said.

What a polite (!) way to start a conversation, thought Diana. But she still couldn't help wondering how bad she must have looked the day before.

"Won't you look at the paintings?"

"As far as I can see, not much has changed in the painting you're working on."

"Doesn't the increase in the wave's rage count as a change?"

"Of course, it counts," Diana said. "Yesterday, the painting was totally different! It's as if I'm looking at another painting now! Wow, I'm amazed! With only a few more brush strokes, you've managed to create a storm that reveals what's inside the wave. Wow, I couldn't be more impressed!"

"The same as yours?"

"Excuse me?"

"The storm in you reveals what's inside pretty well, too."

Struck by his comment, Diana's shoulders sagged. "I'm sorry, I didn't mean to be rude."

"That's okay. What do you really see in the picture?"

"Well… I see you haven't yet added the seagull which is flying in your other paintings."

"You're quite observant, I must say."

"Well, people say so," Diana said.

In spite of his scruffy appearance and crude style of greeting, the artist seemed to be a person of some education.

"Are you a student?" she asked.

He shook his head.

"So you've finished your studies?"

"I was studying economics till I quit."

Diana looked at him as if to say "But why?"

"Before it was too late, I realized I'd never improve my painting by listening to my economics professors."

"Couldn't you work on your painting as well as continue with your studies?"

"It wasn't that I didn't have the time. The problem was that each new painting I finished made me feel that the previous one was better."

"Better in what sense?"

"Well, like every other artist, what I paint onto the canvas is what's inside me. But with every passing day, I could see that my colors were fading. You could perhaps say that I had to leave school for the sake of my original colors."

Diana's eyes showed her approval. "That's quite brave, I must say." She held out her hand to him. "I'm Diana."

The artist just shook her hand.

He had done it again! He'd behaved as if he was indifferent to her. He had neither told her his name nor had the courtesy to say he was glad to meet her. It was pointless to continue an already overextended conversation with someone who wouldn't even bother to give his name. So saying that she had an appointment to keep, Diana muttered goodbye and left.

On her way home, however, her mind was preoccupied with what he had said about the colors fading. Just as the artist had once missed his original colors, Diana thought how much she missed her mother's colors.

12

When Diana had disappeared from view, the beggar waved to the artist. The day before, the artist had gone to him and asked questions about the beautiful girl whose fortune the beggar had told.

The beggar had grinned, saying, "Hold it, son. What happens between me and my customers isn't here to stay; it flies away. You go ask the little lady herself what you figure knowing. She comes here soon. Tomorrow, she comes... But just look at you, asking an old fool like me for help. You are young, art-ist-ic and you are as good-looking as me. What do you need me to charm the little lady for?"

The artist, a little embarrassed, had tried to defend himself. "I saw both of you looking at me, so naturally I wondered why."

"Don't make me laugh, son. Those eyes, big as saucers, see her come down the road there, those big eyes fixing themselves on her, weren't mine, ey? No need for fortune-telling. You wished you meet that little lady the minute you saw her. Do I tell a lie? If that's a lie, let your gull shit on my poor old head!"

Not knowing what to say, the artist had made some excuse and left. He'd realized it wouldn't be easy to pry information out of the old beggar.

Just a few minutes ago, however, when the beggar waved to him with a welcoming smile, the thought passed through his mind that perhaps the beggar had now decided to say something about Diana. The artist would try his luck again by visiting the beggar tonight.

13

In the center of the straw mat, the artist carefully placed the bottle of fruit juice he'd taken from the cooler in his jeep. The beggar had warned him the previous evening not to come empty-handed again. He had also told him to wait until the park was less crowded in order not to chase away potential customers.

"Will you receive a guest now that it's—"

"My place is always open to everybody who doesn't want to know too much."

"Okay, okay, I won't ask so many questions tonight. But I'd like to know how you knew she'd be taking a walk again today. Did you use your fortunetelling? I don't have nine reais by the way, let me say that from the start."

"I don't believe in fortunetelling," the beggar said. "People want to hear their future, so I tell them. What am I supposed to do? Tell them 'Don't ask me, if you live, you find out?'"

"So you mean you actually can't tell fortunes?"

"Beg your pardon, young man, I'm a man of honor. I respect my job. Fortune, that's just the name of the game. Ashes, jars, water, they're just the excuse. You must have some kind of a show for folks, something like they see in the movies. Suppose, everything you say come true, they won't believe it, not without the hokey pokey. Like I said, fortunetelling is just the name. What I do is read faces. I read faces, all right, everything's written there."

"What do you mean?"

"Let's suppose, I watch the little lady when you were talking to her. You know what I see? I see on her face she likes your pictures. Ho-cus po-cus, I know sometime soon she comes back. There, that's fortunetelling for you."

"You're not telling me her walk was an excuse to see me, are you?"

The beggar shrugged his shoulders. "What do I know about little lady's thoughts. I'm not a shrink. Reasons I don't know, I know just results. But leave that now and tell me about yourself. Okay, the little lady is pretty and all, but tell me who *you* are or aren't. Where you're coming from, where you're going to? Some kind of wanderer shows on your face?"

"Yeah, something like that. I've come from Paranagua and I'm working my way back there, painting along the beach. The painting you see right there, that's the first one of my summer project. In fact, according to my plan, I should have finished it yesterday and be 30 miles away at my second pitch by now, but... Anyway, you know the rest."

"The picture doesn't want to be finished after you saw the little lady, eh? Oh my, the chase is always the sweetest. It's when you catch or get caught, things go kind of sour, hey? It's good, son, all good. Let the painting hang around a bit longer."

The beggar emptied his takings for the day out of the coin mug onto the mat. Filling the mug with fruit juice, he set it in front of the artist. He himself took a swig from the bottle.

"That Paranagua of yours, what is it like for begging?"

"I have no idea. And I can't say it is really 'my' Paranagua. I'm from Sao Paulo, originally. I was at college in the US for a while, Boston to be precise, until I quit. Then I moved to Paranagua to live with a friend of mine."

"What do your folks say about you quitting college? I hear college guys make big bucks, eh?"

"My family never had any financial expectations from me. They're doing quite okay. But they did expect more of me than that. They thought I might make a good banker or something along those lines. And because it was Harvard I quit, they did make quite a fuss about it. But there was no other way; I just had to paint."

"Har-vard, huh? My, my! Heard about that place. You told that to the little lady, I bet."

"No."

The beggar stared strangely at the artist.

"Son, there are three choices: 1- You are a fool. 2- You don't want to charm the little lady. 3- You are a fool. Take your pick."

The artist smiled.

"What do you want, son?" the beggar asked, "you want her take you for a loser? A shepherd herding a flock of pictures that don't sell? You tell her who you are. How's she to know who you are if you don't show?"

"I don't know, I'm not sure whether I want her to look at me differently just because I went to Harvard. I don't want to be punished in the end with being loved for other than who I am."

"What?! Who's loving what and punishing who?"

"If she's going to like me because I went to Harvard, it's better she not like me at all. 'Cause I'm not my education. Or my job, or my brains… And I'm not the sum of all of these, either."

"So you know who you are, son?"

"Well, I'm just… I'm just who I am."

"Son, you come listen to me. Don't you see how smart she is with her cool shades pushed way up on her head. That word, 'Harvard,' it'd be music to her ears. Just tell her 'Har-vard,' maybe you'll get lucky."

The artist shook his head. "No, too risky... There will always be someone better than me. But there isn't anyone like me. You know, everyone's fingerprints are different. I like to think we have a kind of inner fingerprint, too. The fingerprint which we cover by wearing trendy gloves..."

"Oh my! Poor kid started talking about gloves now."

"Sorry," the artist said smiling.

"So, what do you expect from the little lady?"

"I don't know. Do you think she'll be here tomorrow?"

"Sorry, son. Fortunetelling, that is worth nine reais. Can't tell it for free to those who don't know what they want."

"I guess you're right."

After a short silence, "Well," the artist said. "I think I should be on my way."

"As you like, son. Bring us guarana next time you come. Jumbo size, mind you."

After putting his paintings into the jeep, the artist stretched out on a lounger under the stars. The light of the full moon was reflected on the water, its path growing wider as it stretched away toward the horizon.

He fixed his eyes on the view, wondering how he could have been so taken by a girl whose face lacked the light he was looking for.

14

At the end of a long, routine, aimless day, Diana was sitting staring at her mother's photograph.

"Mom, let's suppose I did change my mind and went looking for Maria. What difference would that make? Do you really think we can reach Maria just through a name, the name of a woman who supposedly taught her how to talk with roses so many years ago?"

Her chest heaved. "Let's just, for a minute, suppose I traveled thousands of miles to the country where that palace is, and let's suppose I found that woman's guesthouse near that palace. Do we even know if that woman is still alive? If she is, will she remember the foreign girl who came to her guesthouse so many years ago? Well, if she really taught Maria to talk with roses, I'm sure she will. But we don't really think such a thing is possible, do we, Mom?

"And even if she does remember her, what good would that do? How would she know where Maria is now?

"If I really did go there, I'd ask her politely, 'Excuse me, madam, I don't know if you recall but, a long time ago, a girl stayed here. Her name was Maria. Remember? She was the little girl you taught to talk with roses… Now please tell me, where can I find her?'

"What do you think she'd do, Mom, after hearing me ask her that question? Most probably she'd first give me a smile, but when I persisted in asking the same question to the staff and even the guests, she'd politely ask me to leave. And when I told her I wouldn't budge an inch until I'd learned where Maria was, reluctant to throw me out by force, she'd inform the Brazilian Embassy. But I wouldn't give up. I'd keep the people from the embassy busy for hours, asking them, 'Where's Maria? Where's Maria? Where *is* Maria?'

"And then what? I suppose, thinking that I must have lost my mind, they'd send me home on the first available flight with a report in my hand saying I was crazy. At the airport, there'd be men in white coats waiting to take me by the arm and escort me to the nearest mental institution.

"Well, that'd be good news, Mom. Because that's the *only* place I can find Maria."

15

It was as if all the tall, chestnut-haired girls in Rio had convened in the park and as if they'd all agreed to look like Diana. As soon as they got nearer, however, the artist was once again left disappointed. For the past two evenings he'd waited for Diana in the same place, but she hadn't shown up.

He scolded himself for not keeping to his program all for the sake of a girl whom he knew wasn't right for him, but he just couldn't get himself to leave the park.

For a long time now, ever since he'd lost confidence in the trial-and-error approach to love affairs, the artist hadn't been involved in a relationship. In time, he'd come to the realization that each new relationship inevitably meant a new separation, so he'd decided to seek refuge in the turbulence-free nature of being single.

Previously, he'd regarded every parting as a preparation for the next relationship and hadn't thought that he'd lost anything. But soon, he'd come to understand that the ruins of a previous relationship were carried over into the next one.

He'd also realized that most people thought they were the ones who had been wronged when a relationship ended. They all thought they'd given much of themselves while their partner hadn't responded in the same way.

This had been the case for both him and his last girlfriend when they'd parted three years ago. For weeks he'd tried to understand this discrepancy. How could it be that both parties believed they were the ones who'd been wronged? One day, as he was watching two seagulls flying, he found the answer he'd been looking for.

That day, he set up his easel on the cliffs, a short distance from where he lived. As he was absorbed in his painting, a seagull distracted him by taking off from a nearby cliff and diving down toward the water. Immediately, another seagull followed, launching itself from the cliff opposite, swooping down seawards toward the same place. Just as both were a hair's breadth from the water, in danger of colliding, a series of maneuvers took them up into the sky again. As if embracing each other with their wings, they rose in concert to a height far above the level of the cliffs they'd taken off from.

As he watched the flight of these two seagulls, the artist thought that perhaps to be attached, first one needed to become unattached.

However, most people entered into new relationships carrying all their old ties with them. Whether what they carried from the past were feelings of mistrust, being misunderstood, or a defensive wall, those old ties prevented them from living the new relationship freely. Maybe they were right in thinking they had been wronged in their previous relationships; but what they failed to see was that it wasn't their partner who'd wronged them but their own past which they hadn't been able to leave behind.

These two seagulls coming from different cliffs had been able to leave their "past" place and descend to sea level, to "zero" for each other, freeing themselves of their separate identities; so they could rise up into the sky one-in-one.

The artist's habit of painting seagulls dated from that day. But for some time now his seagull had grown tired of solo flights and longed for the moment when he would descend toward the sea. Perhaps this wasn't the right shore for him to do that, yet he still couldn't leave but continued circling the sky.

When it became quite dark, the artist realized that Diana wouldn't be coming to the seafront that night, either.

16

Her dreams did not even let Diana complete a half-hour afternoon nap. She tried to rid her mind of fragmented scenes of a palace and a rose garden. It was impossible. If she couldn't get them out of her head, she wished she could at least make sense of them. But that seemed impossible as well.

She got up and put on her tracksuit and sneakers. Perhaps a short walk in the park or a brief chat with the artist might help.

The old beggar, sitting on his mat with an air more of a king than a beggar, immediately began to count his coins when he saw Diana coming. It was as if he was trying to show that he didn't intend to notice her today, either. Diana didn't care. She no longer expected any explanations from him anyway.

The artist was in his usual place, again busy with his painting.

"Well, how are your colors today?" Diana asked.

"Good. How about yours?"

"Okay, I guess, Senhor so-and-so."

"Jon or Mathias. You choose."

"You have two names?"

"Kind of split personality, if you like."

"How do you mean?"

"Mathias wants to stay in this world and be indulged in it. Whereas Jon wants to fly away."

"Fly where?"

"I don't know, beyond this world, maybe."

"Oh, I see… Mathias, unusual name around here."

"Well, people say so," Mathias said, just as Diana had the last time they talked.

Diana smiled and turned to look at the painting. Since there was still no seagull in the picture, she could tell that it wasn't finished. Although she stared at it for some time, she couldn't think of anything to say about it.

Her silence and the possibility of her leaving made Mathias uneasy. To get to know her better, not only had he changed his schedule, but for days he'd had to stay in a cheap motel—the kind where the shower runs cold, the toilet doesn't flush and the bed is lumpy and narrow.

"Well," Mathias said, "as you can see, I lack inspiration today. I was thinking of going for a coffee at the café over there for a change of scene. Would you care to join me?"

Diana hesitated before saying with an air of indifference, "Well, I suppose I could. I need a break to catch my breath anyway."

Mathias placed his brush carefully into its slot on the easel. "Let's go."

When they got closer to the café, he realized it was a much fancier place than he'd initially anticipated or would have wished for.

17

They arrived at a place with leather-topped tables, torches lit with special lighting effects and copper-coated fire extinguishers in the corners. The kind of place where customers would be eager to pay R$ 25 to drink a cup of coffee perched on uncomfortable wrought-iron chairs while listening to the hubbub inside. Mathias couldn't imagine himself coming to this place even if he stayed in Rio a hundred years. But unfortunately, he'd seen no other café nearby.

They had hardly sat down at a table by the window when a waiter appeared.

"How may I help you?"

After they had sent him off quickly with an order of French vanilla coffee and an espresso, Mathias looked around the room. "What a place for inspiration!"

"Inspiration, oh well," Diana said. "I myself used to paint at one time. But I must admit, inspiration never visited me. I guess that's the difference between a painter and someone who just paints."

"I don't think inspiration is essential."

"You don't?"

"For me, inspiration shows itself in the time it takes to finish a painting rather than in the painting itself. Some paintings take only a couple of days; others I can't call finished even after working on them for a few years. And there's not that much difference among my paintings, either."

"Oh, right, I was going to ask you about that, why do you always paint the sea? Don't you ever paint anything else?"

"No, not lately. I went through a stormy time a few years ago, and since then, I've just been painting the sea."

"Is it all right if I ask what kind of a storm?"

"It was strange. It all began with the breakup of a relationship I'd had. One day I would feel like chasing anyone who came near me with a baseball bat, the next day, I couldn't do without people. In the end, I decided to pour out my 'waves' onto the canvas as seascapes, hoping that they'd help me to understand myself."

"What about the seagull?"

"Long story. I doubt you'd want to hear it."

"Try me."

"Do I really have to tell it?"

In response to her insistent looks, he began to tell her about the day he'd witnessed the flight of the two seagulls. He didn't go into the details, but Diana could work out the significance of the lone seagull in his paintings.

Placing their coffee carefully on the table, the waiter inquired if that would be all. When they nodded their heads, he bowed and withdrew.

"You're still painting the sea; hasn't your storm come to an end yet?"

"Well it has, but in the meantime I've realized something; I've realized that I always like painting different things."

Diana looked confused. Just a few minutes ago, he'd said he only painted seascapes, but now he was saying that he liked painting different things.

"As I went on painting scenes of the same shore one after the other, I realized the thing I thought changed the least, actually changed the most: the sea."

"Like you?" Diana asked, remembering the connection Mathias had made earlier between himself and the sea.

"Well, like everyone. We all think we see the same person when we look in the mirror each morning. Our friends think they see the same person even when we meet after several years."

"True," Diana said, "And even if they do notice a change, it's usually about things like one's weight or hairstyle..."

"Exactly, they never consider that the person in front of them might have become a new person... I personally think someone can change in even a few days."

Diana lowered her gaze as she thought of how much everything recently had forced her to change.

Mathias gently touched her arm. "I'm sorry, did I say something wrong?"

"No, no. What you said reminded me of something, that's all."

Leaning forward on his elbows, Mathias drew closer to her. "Would you like to talk about it?"

"Well... Maybe later."

The waiter reappeared to ask if there was anything else they would like. Diana turned to Mathias. "What would you like? I'm going to have some chocolate cookies."

"Yes, that sounds great, I'll have chocolate cookies, too."

"I'm so sorry," the waiter said. "I've just served cookies to another table, so I happen to know there are only two chocolate cookies left. And that's only one serving. How would it be if I divide the chocolate cookies between you and add a vanilla one to each to complete the serving?"

Reluctantly, they both agreed.

18

The cookies still hadn't arrived. But the two were too deep in conversation to complain. Nevertheless, Mathias still wanted to remind the waiter so they wouldn't lose their chocolate cookies to another customer. Just then, the waiter came to the table carrying two plates.

Taking a bite of her vanilla cookie, Diana asked Mathias, "What are your goals? With regard to your painting, I mean."

"I have only one goal and that is to paint."

"I thought goals are about the future, aren't they?"

"The future," Mathias smiled. "Well, there's a saying I like, 'As long as time flows forward, the future which we are so mesmerized by is nothing but an untouched past.'"

He wondered what Diana would make of this as he took his first bite out of his chocolate cookie.

After a moment of silence, "I suppose what you mean is," Diana said, "a day in the future becomes the 'past' with respect to the day which follows. And that following day is sure to come, because time flows forward... So each day we see as the 'future,' in reality, is nothing but a delayed 'past.' A past that isn't yet touched by time... Did I get it right?"

"I've never met anyone who put it better."

"But all that seems too philosophical, and I don't think it has any practical value in everyday life."

"Hey," he said smiling. "I just tried to answer your question."

"Oh, sorry."

"Actually, all I want to say is that I'd like to achieve my goals in the only time which really exists, that is, in the present. And that's why I've chosen painting as my only goal."

"But you must surely have some long-term plans?"

"Yeah, I do have a plan. I'm planning to work my way back to the small town I live in, near Paranagua, by painting scenes all along the coast. At the end of summer, I'll hold an exhibition at one of the places I've painted."

So Mathias wasn't from Rio... Actually she'd already guessed that. Yet the way Mathias said "the small town I live in near Paranagua," just like that, as if he was saying something of no importance, awoke a familiar feeling in Diana. Loneliness.

"And," Mathias said interrupting her thought. "I've even planned a name for the exhibition, 'The Changing Seas of Brazil.'"

"Sounds good."

"But I don't really know if I'll be able to finish this project on time. And there are many other things I don't know. If I finish the project on time, will I have enough funds for an exhibition? And if I do, will I be able to find a suitable place for it; if I do, will I be able to get permission from the relevant authorities; if I do, will I be able to afford the publicity for it; if I can, will anyone show any interest in my paintings? If they do, will that satisfy me? Even if everything goes perfectly as planned, will I be happy? If I am happy, for how long will it last? Even if it lasts a long time, will I be able to overcome the fear that some day I'll lose it? And the list of things I can't know goes on and on—"

"And on..." chimed in Diana.

"You see, that's why I've decided that to paint is my only goal."

"So, let's say the exhibition actually happens, where's it going to be?"

"I don't know yet; I'd decided before I set out that I'd have it wherever I painted the best painting."

They'd each finished their first cookie. Diana was left with a chocolate cookie on her plate and Mathias with a vanilla one. The difference in the order they'd chosen to eat their cookies had attracted Diana's attention. She had kept the one she liked best till last whereas Mathias had eaten his favorite one first.

It's my turn now, thought Diana. "Look," she said, pointing to the chocolate cookie left on her plate, "this cookie also shows that the future mesmerizes me more. Ever since I was little I've always kept the food I liked best till last. But then, most of the time, when I come to eat it, I find I'm too full. That's what's happened today, too, I'm afraid."

"You're too full to eat it? So I guess your chocolate cookie is left in the past as 'untouched'?"

They both smiled, looking at each other until each felt the need to turn their gaze away.

Diana looked at her watch. "Oh, it's getting late."

Mathias asked for the bill.

"Diana, it's up to you, but if there's anything you'd like to talk about, I'm here to listen."

Diana's eyes clouded over for a minute. Then, regaining her composure, she began to summarize what she'd been living through during the past few months.

Mathias listened with full attention as Diana told her story. When she was finished, he didn't know how to respond. All he could say was, "I'm so sorry."

"What upsets me the most is the idea that my mother doesn't exist anymore," Diana continued. "It's even worse than being left without a mother. I wish she still existed somewhere even if I never saw her or heard her voice."

Mathias noticed the tears in her eyes.

"Diana," he said softly. "I can never realize your suffering. Nobody can. So whatever I say won't mean much… I know it's not the same, but after my grandmother passed away, I was quite upset. Just didn't know how to accept it. But then, I read a little story in a book. It really touched me."

Diana, remembering the stories her mother used to tell her, could hardly hold back her tears.

"I'd like to hear it."

"Well," Mathias said. "There was once a wave in the ocean, rolling along, enjoying the warmth of the sun and the swiftness of the breeze. It smiled at everything around it as it made its way toward the shore. But then, it suddenly noticed that the waves in front of it, one by one, were striking against the cliff face, being savagely broken to pieces. 'Oh God!' it cried. 'My end will be just like theirs. Soon I, too, will crash and disappear!' Just then another wave passing by saw the first wave's panic and asked, 'Why are you so anxious? Look how beautiful the weather is, see the sun, feel the breeze...' The first wave replied, 'Don't you see? See how violently those waves before us strike against the cliff, look at the terrible way they disappear. We'll soon become nothing just like them.' 'Oh, but you don't understand,' the second wave said. 'You're not a wave. You're a part of the ocean.'"

The story and the compassion she'd seen in Mathias' eyes as he'd told it gave Diana a glimmer of comfort. She suddenly felt like reaching out her hand to touch his where it rested on the table. But she stopped herself and gave an appreciative nod instead.

The waiter appeared with the bill tucked inside an oyster shell. When Diana motioned to take it, Mathias said, "Please, I invited you."

As Diana accompanied Mathias to the park, she suddenly remembered the words of the beggar. "That girl just like you, she get to meet that artist some day," he had said. For a moment, she thought of telling this to Mathias and warning him not to mistake Maria for her if their paths should ever cross. But she didn't want to involve the beggar in this, so she decided against it.

When they came to his easel, Diana held out her hand. "I had a lovely time this evening, Mathias. Or Jon. Thanks."

"No, I thank *you*."

For a second, Diana thought of asking him when he was leaving Rio. She would also have liked to tell him that he could find her at the hotel further down the road, and even save him from the cheap motel by offering him a room. But she said goodbye and left without doing any of these.

19

It was past midnight when Diana came down from her art studio. She threw herself carelessly on the bed without a thought for the blue paint spattered all over her. As she'd expected, the bedding became streaked with blue. It's a fair price to pay for painting the sea, she thought.

Actually it wasn't the theme of the painting that was to blame for the mess, but rather the new way of painting she'd tried. She'd begun by throwing aside all the rules she'd ever learned from the art lessons she'd once taken. She'd squeezed a whole tube of blue paint onto her palm, and accompanied by the mystical melodies of Loreena McKennitt, had spread it with both hands in random circles onto the canvas.

Diana felt in some way indebted to Mathias for prompting her to paint again after such a long time. More impor tantly, the story he'd told had made her feel a little better. She didn't want to lose this feeling and wished even to add to it by doing something that would please her mother.

She reached for the green envelope lying in front of the bedside lamp, and read Maria's second letter once again.

Letter No: 2

"The Path in the Garden"

February 22

My Beloved Mother,

In my childhood years, in spite of Others, I was able to preserve my dream of finding you. But as time passed, I could feel my strength fading in the face of their never-ending attempts to turn me into an "other," too.

Then one night, I had a dream. I saw myself in a little wooden boat being driven by the current across the ocean. I was wearing a white nightgown and an orange hat. The horizon was clear, but the boat had neither sail, nor oars to take me there. As I was waiting helplessly, you spoke to me from behind the gray clouds:

"Maria, return to me."

"Where are you, Mom?"

"You have not lost me; I'm always with you."

"Then why can't I see you?"

"Because you are not with me."

"How can I be with you?"

"See me in yourself."

"I can't do that."

"Then try to see me in my gifts."

Suddenly there was a deafening crash as the heavens split open. A hand of light came down and took off my hat, replacing it with a crown of white roses. That hand was your hand, Mom. And that crown was the most beautiful gift I'd ever received.

Looking at its reflection in the water, I admired the beauty of your gift for some time. Then, a huge storm broke out. As the boat rocked this way and that in the middle of towering waves, I crouched down in the bottom of the boat and started to sob, "Help me, Mom!"

A little later, the wind ceased, rain began to fall, and the sea calmed.

When I looked at my reflection in the water again, I saw that my crown was no longer on my head. At that moment, I felt as if everything I had was lost. I felt like a dry river, a wingless bird, a scentless rose... Yet, I was still a river, a bird, a rose. I had to search for my crown immediately.

I searched for it in the boat. I searched for it in the distance, on the sea, and in the sky... But I failed to find it.

I called out to you:

"Mom, where is my crown?"

"Bow your head, Maria."

As soon as I bowed my head, I saw from my reflection that my crown had merely slipped to the back of my head. Then, you spoke to me again. But this time, your voice was not coming from the sky, but coming from the roses in my crown.

"Maria, my child. So that you never think you've lost it, don't search beyond yourself for that which you already have."

Right then, a palace emerged from the middle of the ocean. Near the palace was a garden; its walls were overgrown with roses and from behind them the singing of nightingales was rising.

You spoke to me once more:

"If you want to hear my voice, walk the path in the garden. Hold the gardener's hand and listen to the roses."

"Oh, Mom, it's so far away. There's a whole ocean between us and I don't know how to swim!"

"Don't be afraid, just walk. If you leave your baggage, the water will bear you."

"But I don't have any baggage."

"Believing that the water won't bear you is heavy baggage. So put it down and walk."

"But Mom, where will this path lead me?"

"To Me."

"So I can really be reunited with you in this world?"

"Yes, in this world."

I could never get this dream out of my mind and lived with the hope of its coming true. Three years later, when I was traveling with a friend and her family, I noticed a rose garden hidden at the back of the guesthouse we were staying at. A little further on, I could see Topkapi Palace which seemed very much like the palace I'd seen in my dream. As soon as I saw that garden and the palace, I felt this might be the place you'd wanted me to visit. I wasn't mistaken.

Zeynep Hanim, the lady who owned the guesthouse, was an extraordinary person; she was a "Non-Other." She was the Someone-who-knows I'd been waiting for all along, the one who would help me hear your voice. She took me for magical walks in the rose garden and before long, she taught me what I needed to hear roses. The seeds she sowed in my heart enabled me to hear a rose speak to me years later in my own home.

Hopefully, in my next letter, I will tell you about this third phase of my journey to you.

With all my love...

Maria

It wasn't the first time Diana had read this letter. But this time, she felt a little different. She thought about how her twin had devoted her life to finding her mother. The intensity of the feelings she had for her mother, the never diminishing longing, her determination to find her...

Well, perhaps Maria was fantasizing too much, perhaps in her letters she was talking about the things she wished to live, rather than the ones she actually lived. Maybe she was crazy, or maybe just a lover of fantasy. But one thing was for sure, Maria was in love with her mother... More importantly, Maria had managed to keep her mother alive in her heart for so many years, something Diana found impossible to do.

And now, at a time when Maria thought she was about to meet her mother, she'd lost her forever. Perhaps Maria didn't even know this. Or perhaps it was because she'd learned her mother was going to die that she'd decided to take her own life, just so she could be with her as quickly as possible.

In her dream, her mother had said Maria would see her in *this* world. But the fancied world Maria had built for herself came crashing down as this promise turned out to be a lie. Maria would never be able to see her mother again in this world.

"Just like me," whispered Diana.

20

Mathias had finished his painting at midnight. Yet, he was still in the park as dawn broke, wrestling with the question he'd been unable to answer throughout the night: Should he change the name of his exhibition to 'The Changing Seas of Rio de Janeiro' or not?

The sea along this coast was also constantly changing, so he could rent a small bungalow nearby for the summer and paint all his pictures in the park. It would certainly be interesting. But he was having a hard time making up his mind. Just for the sake of a summer full of inspiration, he didn't want to begin a relationship which he knew wouldn't last.

Walking to his jeep, he grabbed two bottles of coke from the cooler, an action that didn't go unnoticed by the beggar who hadn't yet switched to the sitting position he adopted during his working hours.

"You fool!" the beggar shouted. "Get yourself over here!"

He took the bottle of coke the artist held out to him. "Cola all you got, this early in the day? Jumbo size guarana is what I said."

"You said you read faces, right?"

"If I said so, then it is so. But it isn't for free, son. Let's get that straight."

"Just now, I scribbled down a list of ten qualities. The list is called, 'The kind of girl I'm looking for.' Guess what, she matches item two through item ten. And I thought I hated making calculations."

"What's your list got to do with me, son? What you want from me, spit it out."

"I thought maybe you could tell me something about the first item on my list, which is more important for me than all the rest combined."

"What sort of an item would that be?"

"There should be a light in her face."

"My, my! What sort of light would that be?"

"A light I've never seen in anyone's face before, but which I'll recognize as soon as I see it. Unfortunately, she doesn't have it, either."

"What would this light be good for, son?"

"A sign to tell me that I've found my soul mate."

"What mate?! Don't talk mystery, son. Puzzles aren't for me."

Mathias pointed toward the sea. "Every day thousands of people look at that, at the same thing. Most of them see the sea, but perhaps a few of them may see something different. I wonder if anyone has ever seen a burning desert there? Or a mountain?"

"Oh, my. Don't do it to me, son, don't!"

"If, one day, I claim I see a desert while looking at the sea, or a sea while looking at the desert, would anyone believe me?"

"Oh, no, you did it, son, you did it. Give this old man a break and just say what you're talking about."

"All I'm getting at is, my soul mate is the one who believes me even when the whole world thinks I'm lying. More than that, she's the one who points out to me the sand-dunes I've overlooked or the coves I haven't noticed."

"Stop, stop right there!" the beggar said, making a time-out gesture. "Son, from now on, you'll pay for what you tell this old man. Every word you say without my okay will cost you one whole real!"

Mathias smiled.

"I got just one thing to say to you, son. I'm sorry but, my reading faces got nothing to do with the light you want in the face of your little lady. You think it's easy to find a light in a face? In all this long life, I've seen it just once. On brother Joe's, it was on my brother Joe's face where I saw that light. Real bright it was. Year 1962. Cadillac. Brand new. Metallic, too. Black pearl! Me, while I work on its door, Joe, he keeps his eyes wide open. It seemed we got it made. Then we suddenly hear a few footsteps, so I turn to Joe. That second, my eyes dazzle, okay. All thanks to the cop's 500 Watt flashlight, Joe's face was full of light. Bright, bright light! Our wicked Joe, he was illumined, all right."

Mathias started laughing.

"Son, let's get to the point. You're staying or you're going?"

"What do you think I'm doing here at this time of day? I'm open to any suggestions. But one thing I do know. If I leave, it'll be for good. It's best for both of us not to let it go any further. I've gone too far already. I knew it from the beginning, but I couldn't help it. I chatted with her, invited her for coffee, told her about myself and tried to understand her. Worst of all, I tried to impress her. None of that should have happened. And now, I'm thinking of leaving without even saying goodbye. You tell me, what should I do?"

"Go away, son."

"Go away from you or from the city?"

"Don't ask me what you already know. For me, I say stay, but you say go. Me, I say enjoy yourself, get to know the little lady, take her places, be happy. But you, you set on going. You come to me because you couldn't make yourself say stay. Before you sat down, I saw it in your face, that you'd be gone. That's how I read faces, son. Two big bottles of cola make nine reais, so you were my guest. I'm a man of honor, don't forget, and I respect my job."

After remaining silent for a moment, Mathias held his hand out to the beggar:

"I'll miss our little chats, my friend."

21

“A person can change even within a few days,” Mathias had told her. Was that also true for one day? Could a person who’s sensitive and caring one day, get up and leave the next, without so much as a goodbye?

I’m afraid he could, Diana said to herself, since she hadn’t seen him for the past six evenings.

Having just returned from her evening walk, Diana was riffling through the numbers in her phonebook, wondering how she’d gotten to know so many people. From among all those numbers, she would probably pick one of the girls, invite her over for a coffee and before long, she’d bring the subject to the real issue. Then, she’d hear a few scenarios from her friend highlighting the logical reasons why the artist had gone off just like that. And soon, she would be convinced that the reason was not because he hadn’t been attracted to her, and so her self-image would remain untarnished.

I don't think Maria would act this way, thought Diana.

She threw the phonebook back on the table. Not because she was competing with Maria. She just no longer felt like calling anyone. But she dialed another number, the number of the travel office in the hotel.

"Hello, how may I help you?"

"Hi, Caroline, it's Diana. I'd like to ask you a favor. If I'm not mistaken, Topkapi Palace is in Istanbul, right? After you check on that, can you please book me a flight for Friday? Make it an open return."

"Did I hear correctly, Senhora Oliveira, did you say Friday?"

"Yes, that's what I said."

"But what about your graduation on Sunday, Senhora Oliveira? Has it been postponed?"

"No, but I have to leave right away."

"Everything's all right, I hope?"

"Don't worry, Caroline. Everything is as it should be."

Part Two

22

When the pilot announced that the plane would soon be landing, the letter Diana had read several times during the flight was still in her hand.

Letter No: 3

"Annihilation in the Rose"

March 1

My Beloved Mother,

About a year ago, there was a time when I hardly ate or drank. I lost all interest in the things I'd previously enjoyed. I never left my room and spent most of my time in the company of my roses which had started to release scents I'd never smelled before.

Every corner of my room was filled with the roses I'd begun to grow after coming back from the rose garden. I felt like a florist who couldn't bring herself to sell her roses.

One day, something very strange happened: I heard the roses breathing. This went on for days. Sometimes a fresh breeze would come from them, flowing through my hair as if to sweep away all traces of the past from my mind.

One evening, this breeze became quite strong, increasing even more throughout the night, dying away as dawn was breaking. Suddenly the room was filled with a blinding light. Everywhere was dazzlingly bright, so bright that I couldn't see anything. A deafening silence enveloped the room.

The silence was broken when the pink rose at the head of my bed spoke to me. But it was as if the voice didn't come from the rose, but from me. From inside of me!

The voice grew louder and louder, rising to such a crescendo that I couldn't hear, see, or smell anything. All I could see, all I could smell, all I could touch was the voice of my rose.

I became afraid of myself. No, that couldn't be possible. How could I be afraid of myself? I wasn't even there. There was only the rose. The voice of the rose.

We both spoke with that one voice:

"Peace be with you, Maria."

"I don't believe it! I don't believe I'm hearing a rose!"

"No, Maria, it's because you believed, you can hear me."

"But this is extraordinary!"

"For those who are extraordinary, what's extraordinary is quite ordinary."

"I don't think I'm worthy of such praise."

"That's why you're worthy of it."

"Now that I have heard a rose, can I hear my mother, too?"

"Your mother speaks to you through everything. But it's only after listening to Socrates that you will realize this and hear her voice."

"Where can I find Socrates?"

"You can't find him. He'll find you."

"But when?"

"When the right time comes."

Those were the first and last words I heard from the pink rose. From that day to this, I've been waiting for Socrates to appear; I've been waiting for him just as the fox waited for the Little Prince to come and tame it. Even though your address is right in front of me now, Mom, I know I won't hear your voice until I meet Socrates.

But I'm sure he'll find me. I'm sure because my rose said so. Who knows, maybe I'll meet Socrates in Rio.

Hoping to send you my final letter when I get there.

With all my love…

Maria

23

Diana had waited half an hour at the airport for her luggage which had showed up after everyone else's, and had lost her place in the taxi line twice as rushing people had pushed her aside. She'd had to endure the puzzling language of the chatty driver. She'd failed to convince the vendors at Sultanahmet Square that she didn't need a carpet. And now, worst of all, after diving into every guesthouse looking for a nonexistent garden behind it, she couldn't conceal her tears from people passing by. If only she'd been able to find Zeynep Hanim's guesthouse, none of this would have mattered.

She found a deserted corner in Hagia Sophia and cried. She sat there staring at the walls until closing time. Its walls, though cracked and dilapidated, seemed to be engaged in a noble fight against time to uphold the spiritual remembrance of millions of people. Maybe it was worthwhile to persevere for such a cause. But was it worth it to torment herself in the cause of finding Maria?

When the museum guard warned for a third time, "Museum's closing!" Diana left Hagia Sophia and wandered aimlessly in the direction of Topkapi Palace. On reaching the historic fountain in front of the main entrance to the palace, she sat down on the ground since there was no danger of this place closing.

While she was wondering whether she would be able to find a seat on the next flight home, she heard a voice above her:

"Had a tough day, huh?"

When Diana raised her head, she saw a middle-aged, well-dressed foreign woman who was regarding her half interestedly, half condescendingly, as if she'd never seen anyone sitting in the street before.

"Don't even ask," Diana said. "There isn't a hotel I haven't been in. Now I'm just getting to know the streets."

"Yes, the high season's begun. We also had a hard time finding a room."

The woman pointed to the narrow road winding its way alongside the palace wall. "In fact," she said. "We'd set our hearts on staying in one of the two guesthouses over there, but they were both fully booked. So we had to settle for the Four Seasons, instead."

"Oh!" said Diana, jumping to her feet. "Let me take a look at those guesthouses myself. You enjoy the Four Seasons."

24

Just opposite Diana were two large wooden houses. The one painted champagne was bigger, and as far as appearance was concerned, it looked more luxurious. It had a garden entrance. The other house was painted pastel green. As its entrance was on the street, she couldn't work out whether there was a garden at the back or not.

Diana was eager to rush into one of them; but because she was unable to picture Zeynep Hanim in her mind, she couldn't decide which of the houses might be hers. If in fact, either of them were.

She chose to try the larger one first. As she walked toward the entrance, she inspected the garden. Although there was a variety of flowers of all colors—yellow, pink, blue, purple, crimson, orange—she couldn't see a single rose. Retracing her steps, she entered the second house through a narrow doorway.

Inside, the receptionist was busy on the phone. After waiting exactly seventeen minutes for him to finish his conversation, Diana finally gave up, and stopped one of the passing waiters. Pronouncing every syllable with care, she asked, "Is Zeynep Hanim here?"

"She went out half an hour ago, madam. But she said she would be back within an hour."

Surprised, Diana hesitated for a moment.

"Oh… Okay… When she comes back, would you please tell her there's someone who'd like to see her?"

"Certainly, madam. If you like, you may wait in our tea-room."

I didn't expect it to be that easy, Diana thought. It was as if fate, which had been against her up to now, had suddenly decided to lend a hand.

25

The tearoom, consisting of four separate seating areas, was well-lit and furnished in authentic Turkish style. Apart from the waiter in his gold-braided vest at the entrance, there was no one else around.

Kilims in plain patterns of brick-red, mustard yellow and blue, decorated the dark parquet floor. The walls were hung with paintings depicting various scenes of old Istanbul: Ottoman boats on the Golden Horn, mosques with their minarets vying with each other to reach the sky, ceremonies of whirling dervishes, grand wooden houses stretching along the shores of the Bosphorus…

Within a short while, the sound of approaching footsteps roused Diana from her reverie in front of the paintings.

Into the tearoom, came a woman with delicate features and big blue eyes, her hair, graying in places, done in a chignon at the back of her head, and her perfect complexion belying her age. The long white linen dress she wore gave her an air of distinction.

When their eyes met, the elderly woman had already opened her arms and was rushing toward Diana:

"My goodness, I can't believe my eyes! Maria, it's you! Oh, what a beautiful young lady you've become!"

Zeynep Hanim embraced her in such a way that, for a moment, Diana was reminded of her mother. Whenever her mother had embraced her, Diana had always felt it wouldn't be her mother who'd let go first.

"Oh, let me have a look at you," Zeynep Hanim said, taking Diana's face in her hands.

"I'm sorry, but I'm not Maria," said Diana, pulling away. "My name is Diana."

Zeynep Hanim smiled. "Maria, how could I ever forget you?"

"No, really, I'm not her. I'm her twin."

Zeynep Hanim regarded her doubtfully. "Maria, my dear, but you have no twin."

"Please, you must believe me. Actually, I've come here to ask *you* about Maria."

"What do you mean? Surely it was you who phoned me the other day and said you'd be coming here this week."

"What? Did, did Maria call you? She said she was coming here? Where's she now?"

Zeynep Hanim motioned Diana toward a chair as if trying to calm her down. Sitting in the chair opposite, she asked, "So you're definitely not Maria?"

"You can take my word for it. But please tell me, where's Maria, when is she arriving here?"

"It's not that I don't believe you, my dear, but—"

"Please, when will Maria come?"

"She didn't say exactly which day she'd arrive, but she should be here within the next three or four days. I have no idea where she is now. It's been many years since I saw her. And it was the very first time she called since then. But what about you? Haven't you seen her recently?"

"It's a long story, but if you're willing to listen, I'm here to share it with you."

"Of course, I'd like to hear it. But first tell me what you'd like to drink. Are you hungry? You may order as you like. I'll have some green tea with fresh mint. I recommend it."

"Thank you, an espresso would be fine for me."

"Well, we have espresso, but perhaps you'd like to try a cup of Turkish coffee?"

"Why not."

On hearing the order, the waiter left the room.

26

By the time the waiter came back bearing a silver tea tray, Diana had finished telling Zeynep Hanim all that had happened.

"I'm so sorry, Diana," Zeynep Hanim said, placing her hand over Diana's. "But don't worry about Maria. Maria isn't someone who'd harm herself... But, my dear, what about you? You must have been going through a really tough time."

"I'm trying to pull myself together. But to be able to do that, first I have to find Maria. I need your help. If she calls again, I'd really prefer it if you wouldn't tell her about me until she gets here, if that's okay? Also, if you can find out her phone number or where she is, I'd be very happy to know."

"If she phones, sure, I'll do what I can. I'm so glad you're going to meet her, Diana. Maria is an extraordinary girl. It's sad you haven't known each other all these years."

Zeynep Hanim picked up the silver teapot and filled the crystal glass in front of her. She checked to see whether Diana was enjoying her coffee before asking, "What did Maria say about me in her letters?"

On hearing this, Diana suddenly felt strange. In the excitement of learning that Maria would be coming there, the question of what kind of a person Zeynep Hanim might be had completely slipped her mind. Wasn't she the one who'd taught Maria how to speak with roses?!

She took another careful look at Zeynep Hanim. With her smiling eyes, the peaceful expression on her face, the softness in her manners and her tone of voice, she seemed not only sane, but resembled the very picture of a perfect lady. Most probably, she would smile out of sympathy when she heard what Maria had said about her and comfort Diana by explaining why her twin had written such things in her letters.

"I know it will probably sound funny to you," Diana said, "but in one of her letters Maria wrote that you'd taught her to hear roses speak."

Contrary to her expectations, Zeynep Hanim looked not the least bit surprised.

Diana wanted to hear her say that "hearing roses speak" was nothing but a game she'd played with Maria. Or that the things Maria talked about in her letters were mere expressions of her great imagination. This was the kind of explanation Diana wanted to hear because she would feel very uneasy sitting with a person who wouldn't deny the idea that she could teach people how to hear roses.

"So that's what Maria wrote," Zeynep Hanim said eventually. "It's unbelievable, isn't it?"

Diana didn't know what to make of this question. It was on the tip of her tongue to say, "Yes, it's absolutely unbelievable," but at the last moment she changed her mind and decided rather to sound out Zeynep Hanim.

"Isn't reality unbelievable, too?" Diana said calmly. "Take the Earth for example, it feels so stable under our feet, but it's actually moving more rapidly than the fastest plane."

Zeynep Hanim made no comment. Realizing that she wouldn't say anything, Diana finally asked, "Did you really teach Maria to hear roses?"

Zeynep Hanim took a sip of her tea. "Diana, be my personal guest until Maria arrives. Here, we also serve people who can't hear roses. And I'm sure all the staff will feel honored to serve Maria's twin."

Diana wondered if Zeynep Hanim was just trying to shield Maria. Or maybe Diana was faced with a person who just enjoyed seeming mysterious. Or was there a completely different reason behind Zeynep Hanim's behavior?

"Thank you, but I can't accept that. However, I'd like to stay until Maria arrives if you have a room I can pay for."

"I'm sorry, Diana, the house is fully booked. The only way I can help you is if you agree to be my personal guest."

Zeynep Hanim beckoned to the waiter, and said something to him in Turkish before turning to Diana.

"My dear, you look tired. If you like, someone can take you straight up to your room. If there's anything you want, just ask at reception. In any case, we'll be seeing each other again when Maria gets here."

Although Zeynep Hanim was being kind, Diana could sense that she was disappointed that it wasn't Maria sitting in front of her. For a moment, she thought of leaving after saying, "Thanks a lot, but I don't want your room or your hospitality on Maria's account."

But instead, she nodded in acceptance of Zeynep Hanim's offer.

27

After a night of undisturbed sleep, Diana was down to breakfast early. As she entered the breakfast room, she saw Zeynep Hanim sitting by herself at a table near the door.

Diana took a deep breath in anticipation of what she was about to do. She wasn't going to do this because she believed in Maria's fantasies or because she wanted to please Zeynep Hanim. Her only objective was to better understand how Maria had become the way she was.

"Excuse me, I hope I'm not disturbing you," Diana said.

"No, my dear, but I was just about to leave."

Diana took another deep breath and in a resolute manner, she said, "I would like you to teach me what you taught Maria."

Zeynep Hanim looked at her in silence. It was as if this look penetrated into Diana's mind, reading all her thoughts and feelings, before leaving her once again alone with herself.

"Won't you sit down, Diana?"

"Does this mean you agree?"

"Agree to what?"

She's just acting as if she didn't understand, Diana thought. Maybe she wanted to seem even more mysterious. Diana had to beat her at her own game.

"I want you to teach me to hear roses just like you taught Maria."

"Why do you want me to do this?"

"Well, it must be an incredible experience to have affected Maria so much."

The soft expression on Zeynep Hanim's face, which always seemed about to give way to a smile, suddenly vanished.

"And do you think it'll be worth what I will require in return?"

"What is that?" Diana asked.

"I want you to kill yourself."

Diana was uncertain whether this was a joke or just another piece of the puzzle. So she said nothing, only laughed. She expected Zeynep Hanim to laugh as well, but she didn't.

"Did you ask Maria for the same thing?"

"There was no need. Maria didn't have a self which doubted that roses could speak or be heard. What about you, Diana, do you have such a self? Do you believe you can hear roses or do you doubt it?"

"Oh, please! When Maria came here, she was only a child. When I was that age, I believed in things which were even more unbelievable than talking roses."

"Such as?"

"Such as, such as… I believed I could swim around the world, for example. I believed I could fly or talk with angels… My mother used to tell me that my father was with God. So I promised myself to swim all around the world to find the place where God and my father lived. If I couldn't find my father anywhere in the sea, then I was going to put on the biggest pair of wings to search for him in the sky. And if I couldn't find him there, either, I would ask an angel to take me to him. Why? Because I was a child! Do you know what the truth about my father was; where he was when I was dreaming of doing all these?"

Diana stopped, ready to burst into tears. "Oh, never mind, it doesn't matter anymore."

"And then what happened, Diana?"

"What do you mean, what happened?"

"When did you give up searching for your father or dreaming you would see him again? Who taught you that there was no way you could find him?"

Diana got to her feet. "I'm sorry, but this was a mistake. My mistake. I won't bother you again."

"Just as I thought," Zeynep Hanim said. "Diana is unwilling to die, so she'll never be able to hear the roses."

Turning her back on Zeynep Hanim, Diana marched toward the door. But she still heard the question whispered from behind her:

"Who do you think understands the value of life the most, Diana?"

Diana stopped and waited without turning her head.

"Those who have tasted death," said Zeynep Hanim.

Diana returned to the table. "Please tell me, what is it you want from me?"

"Just one thing: Kill the self within you that doesn't believe you can hear roses. Tasting such a death will grant you a life in which you can hear them. And I'm only asking you to do this because you wanted me to teach you how to hear roses."

"Well, let me be honest with you," Diana said, "if this thing, this so-called 'hearing roses,' is what I think it is, that is, if you're suggesting that one can hear them physically, I don't believe it's possible. And any claim to the contrary doesn't awaken the slightest curiosity in me. But if, in spite of this, you say you can teach me, then please do."

"But there are some conditions," Zeynep Hanim said.

"Like what?"

"Very simple. You'll do exactly what you're told. You're free to give up the lessons any time, but as long as you go on with them, you must do exactly what I say. The lessons will take place at the assigned times in the garden at the back of the house. You must not be a second late. It's better not to come at all than to be late. In the garden, the gardener's word, my word to be precise, is law. There will be four lessons in all. During this time, which could be viewed as an internship for the art of hearing roses, you're forbidden to go out of the guesthouse unaccompanied. I have one more condition: a blank résumé."

"Blank résumé?"

"Naturally, you have the résumé of a young woman who was born at a specific time, in a specific place, into a specific social environment. If you'd been born in Rio de Janeiro a few centuries later or had been raised by Red Indians a few centuries earlier or grown up on an island in the South Pacific today, your life experience would have been completely different. Perhaps, if not certainly, you would have a totally different perception and understanding of life, maybe quite the opposite of the one you have now.

"Résumés are all relative. But we hear roses with a part of ourselves which is not bounded by time, place, or the social environment in which we live. That's why you have to wipe out all sections from your résumé—education, past experience, and especially, the reference section. If these things had been of any use in a rose garden, botanists would have been the first to hear roses. What you've learned up to now will only be baggage for you here. And heavy baggage, too."

Suddenly, Diana looked at Zeynep Hanim as if she'd remembered something. "And the water won't bear me with this baggage, right?"

"Very true. Where did you hear that?"

"According to one of Maria's letters, my mother said almost the same thing to her in a dream. But then, Maria says that a lot of what she saw in her dream came true later."

"That's only natural," Zeynep Hanim said. "Dreams are the leaven of reality."

Unwilling to talk any longer about Maria's dreams, "Well," Diana said. "We were speaking of the conditions...

Suppose I agree to keep to all of them, what do I get in return?"

"Whatever your intention is in entering the garden, that's what you'll get. It's not what you do in the garden which matters, but *why* you do it. If your intention in learning to hear roses is simply to make you different from other people, I'm afraid you'll only gain vanity. If your intention is just to hear roses, you'll hear roses. Or like Maria, if you enter the garden to hear your mother's voice through the roses, you'll hear her voice. If, apart from these, what you want is to experience something new for entertainment, that's also possible at your own expense."

Everything was like a joke. This elderly lady, who until a little while ago had seemed to be a soft-natured person, had suddenly turned into a total quality-control manager who'd forgive no mistake, or an army general showering his aide-de-camp with orders, as if the subject she was lecturing on with such earnestness wasn't about hearing flowers, birds and bees!..

"I'm intrigued about something," Diana said. "Whether one believes in it or not, the idea of hearing roses sounds quite sensational. But, on the other hand, the conditions you listed and your approach, well... Don't, don't get me wrong, but it all seems very rigid and confining."

"Rain clouds, rain, water; all these are sensational, too. But to quench our thirst, ultimately we need a confining glass."

Diana remained silent for a while before asking, "You said only four lessons, right?"

"Right, only four."

"Well, okay then."

Zeynep Hanim got to her feet. "Our first lesson will begin tomorrow morning at 6:11. Our subject is the Mathematics of Hearing Roses. You don't need to bring books with you on algebra or geometry or anything of that sort. Just be on time by the stools at the entrance to the garden, that'll be enough."

"At 6:11 in the morning?!"

"Precisely."

Although Diana wasn't enchanted by the idea of getting up that early, she nodded in agreement.

"Good. Now let's synchronize our watches," Zeynep Hanim said. "Oh, I nearly forgot. If you manage to hear a rose upon completion of our lessons, a reward will be waiting for you."

"You really see a chance for that to happen, don't you? You must have great faith in me."

"As long as you have faith in yourself, I have faith in you."

"So what's the reward?"

"A prized saying that has come down through the centuries."

"What if I can't succeed?" Diana asked with a wry smile. "Isn't there any punishment for failing the class?"

"The silence of roses," Zeynep Hanim said. "Not being able to hear roses is enough of a punishment for those who fail to hear them."

28

Diana sat down on one of the stools. There were still five minutes left until the time set by Zeynep Hanim for the lesson. The wooden fence around the garden was taller than Diana, preventing her from seeing over it. In contrast to the high fence, the door to the garden was exceptionally low.

Her eyes were fixed on the minute-hand of her watch, her mind busy wondering what the mathematics of hearing roses could mean. However far she stretched her imagination, she had no idea what the content of this bizarre mathematics lesson might be.

The moment the hand of her watch touched eleven minutes past the hour, she heard Zeynep Hanim's voice:

"It's not something you can grasp with your intellect."

Diana smiled to conceal her feeling of surprise. Despite the way it appeared, she didn't think Zeynep Hanim could have read her mind. What else would a person be wondering about other than the lesson, waiting here at this crazy hour, counting the minutes to be taught how to hear roses?

"If it's something my intellect can't grasp, then you tell me what hearing roses is all about."

"Have you ever eaten an olive?" Zeynep Hanim asked.

"Of course. Why?"

"Well, I was wondering if you could explain to me what an olive tastes like… Let's make a deal. If you can describe to me the taste of an olive, I'll describe to you what it's like to hear a rose."

"Very well," Diana said. "An olive… it's… it's salty… well… it's like… oily… tastes like… well… it's kind of strong… It's like…"

Zeynep Hanim wrinkled her nose. "Ooow, I've got a salty, oily, strong taste in my mouth. Fortunately I've eaten olives before, otherwise, after your description, I would never try them."

"Okay, okay, you win," Diana said.

"Well, let's put the taste of an olive or hearing roses aside now, and before we step into the garden, let's get this math lesson out of the way, shall we?"

"Please, go ahead, I'm listening."

"The mathematics of hearing roses is a lesson that must certainly be studied by everyone whether one believes in the art of hearing roses or not. Simply because, the equation you'll learn in this lesson is applicable to any question which has an innumerable number of possible answers but which can't be answered by any of our five senses. Say, for example, a question like 'What happens after death?'

"Now, before we're tempted to give an answer to such a question, we should bear this equation in mind: One divided by infinity ($1/\infty$). I'll take that up in a minute. But first, tell me, do you hear the song the roses are singing right now?"

"You know perfectly well that I don't hear any such thing."

"Which song are they singing, Diana?"

"I told you, I don't hear anything."

"Come on, just make a guess. Perhaps you'll hit on the right one."

Realizing that Zeynep Hanim wasn't going to let go, Diana said, "All right, fine. They're singing 'Purple Rain.'"

"Do you think you guessed the right answer?"

"Of course not."

"I'll give you one more chance. Take another shot."

"Fine. 'Morning Has Broken' by Cat Stevens."

"Do you think you have it right this time?"

"Of course not. May I ask what you're getting at?"

"Now, let's test your knowledge of statistics a little. So, tell me, what are the chances of your ever guessing the song right?"

"Next to nothing."

"Exactly. Dividing the number of songs being sung by the number of possible answers gives us the probability of arriving at the correct song by means of guessing. The number of songs being sung is 1. If you think of the songs which have been written all over the world for thousands of years, in hundreds of languages, by millions of songwriters, the number of possibilities can be counted in the trillions. And if we add to that number the songs which haven't yet been written but which are known to the roses, then we can say that we have an infinite number of possible answers. In that case, the probability of arriving at the correct song is 1 divided by infinity. And that's the equation we have to know before we can learn how to hear roses. So, what's 1 divided by infinity?"

"Zero, as far as I remember."

"Right, but if it were the usual zero, this would mean there was absolutely no chance that one could know the song which the roses were singing. So, 1 over infinity equals a special zero."

"A special zero?"

"I'm sure your knowledge of mathematics is greater than mine, Diana. But I'd still like to briefly go over the mathematical value of this equation with you.

"Let's take any equation, 1 over some number... As the number by which 1 is divided increases, the number of zeros preceding 1 also increases in the answer to the equation.

If we divide 1 by infinity, in the answer, there will be an infinite number of zeros in front of 1. So, the answer would read as zero point zero zero zero, all the way to infinity. But even if we don't see it, there's always a 1 remaining at the far end of the answer. It's zero, yet, a special zero that ends with a 1, even if it's concealed in infinity.

"Now, this is very important. While the equation tells us that the probability of knowing the correct song by means of guessing is zero, it hints that it's not impossible to arrive at the correct answer, because there's a 1 at the end.

"When I asked you what song the roses were singing, you responded in the best way by saying you didn't know. Why? Because you knew that you couldn't know. You were able to see that, by means of guessing, it would be pointless to try to answer a question which has innumerable possible answers and which can't be answered by using the five senses.

"So the Real Song can't be arrived at by the mere guesses of the intellect, but only by way of *witnessing*. First, we have to understand that we hear roses not with our ears but with our hearts.

"At birth, everyone's heart has this ability. But hearts grow deaf as time goes by. The one who wishes to witness roses sing, must first regain this ability which gets lost while we are being taught to become a grownup. And to regain this is only possible by maintaining a constant interest in the roses and caring for them, by loving them.

"Perhaps we may not hear the roses on our first visits to the garden. But we must never lose hope. First and foremost, a lack of certitude, along with any other negative thoughts or feelings, is our enemy in the garden.

"Imagine a mountain… From the top of this mountain, the view is wonderful. You want to be there, but the summit seems so far away that you lose hope of reaching it. You give up, saying, 'I'll never get there.'

"The truth is, the footsteps of the ones who reached the top were no bigger than yours. But they'd just gone on putting those small footsteps one after the other. It's not miracles which make the impossible happen, it's perseverance. This is how water wears away rocks, and this is how the people of the 21st century hear roses sing.

"If we believe we're capable of hearing them, and if we persevere, then sooner or later we will. It is possible because there's always a 1 hidden at the end of the zeros. And if we follow the path of nothingness till infinity, we'll definitely reach that One."

"What if the roses don't talk at all?" Diana said. "Or they don't sing any songs? Let me tell you the probability of that. If the number of songs the roses sing is zero, the equation becomes zero divided by infinity, and that is equal to zero. And this time, it isn't a special zero but a simple fat zero. Which means there's no song and no possibility of hearing roses."

"True," Zeynep Hanim said. "Two paths. One begins and ends here and now, the other stretches out into infinity.

In answering the question, 'Do roses sing?' or 'Can I hear roses?' we choose one of these two paths. These questions have only two possible answers: 'Yes' or 'No.' There isn't a third answer. For those who say 'Yes,' the solution to the equation is the special zero, whereas for those who say 'No,' it's, as you said, a simple fat zero. That's why there's no possibility for those who say 'No' to ever hear roses sing. This isn't what they're aiming for anyway. For them, it's enough that they hear the sound frequencies picked up by the ear. Any sound beyond that is of no interest to them."

"But who's to decide which answer is right?" Diana asked.

"It doesn't matter which answer is right, Diana. What's important is what you yourself believe in. Ask yourself; say, 'Which do I believe in?' It's as easy as that. If your answer is 'I can't hear roses,' well, that's okay, too. Nobody can blame you for that. There have to be those who don't believe in order for there to be those who do believe. Day exists because there's night, and night exists because there's day. Instead of asking 'Which one is more beautiful, day or night?' ask yourself which one you live in. Ask yourself, 'Do I believe I can hear roses?'

"But you must ask yourself this question. Because if you're sure the answer is 'No,' then you don't ever need to enter the garden. You'll be spared from the difficulties, disappointments, and failures you'll face there. To begin with, you won't have to listen to me. You'll not have to spend days, months, maybe years, waiting in front of a rose hoping to hear it speak. Everything will be much easier, much more comfortable. For example, instead of getting up early to come to the garden, you can stay in bed sleeping for as long as you wish. What do you think, wouldn't that be much more enjoyable?"

Zeynep Hanim paused for a second before she added, "Actually, that would depend on whether you believe you can hear roses or not. Just imagine, for someone who believes that roses can be heard, which would be more enjoyable: Sleeping? Or awakening with the hope of hearing them sing?

"So Diana, are you one of those who say, 'Yes, I can hear roses'?"

Zeynep Hanim waited for sometime for Diana's answer which never came.

"I knew it," Zeynep Hanim said. "The answer you gave is the reason why you're here."

"But I didn't give an answer."

"I heard the answer I needed to hear. Sometimes silence is more convincing than a hundred spoken promises."

Diana remained silent.

"However, believing that roses sing isn't sufficient to know the song they are singing. There are only two ways of knowing what the actual song is. Either you hear it yourself or learn it from someone who does.

"It's much better to hear it yourself, though. Roses have a divine voice. They draw you out of yourself, take you to their world and bring you back permeated with rose scent. This scent then no longer originates from the roses but from within yourself; because you have finally come to realize what it means to be responsible for your rose."

"Wait a minute," Diana said. "That's just the phrase Maria used in the farewell letter to her father. She wrote that she was leaving home because she'd finally understood what it meant to be responsible for a rose. She must have been thinking of coming to you when she wrote that letter. That's why she must have left home."

For a moment, Diana sat lost in thought. Then, "In her letters," she said, "Maria described you as 'Someone-who-knows.' There's something I want to know, Zeynep Hanim. It's something beyond the scope of the five senses, but it has nothing to do with roses..."

"It's about your mother, isn't it?"

"How did you know?"

"Maria wanted to know the same thing. Do as Maria did. While she was here, she prayed to God to give her news of her mother. Even if no one else does, God knows what happened to your mother. Ask and He will answer. Even if you don't hear God, He hears you."

Diana looked unconvinced.

"God doesn't leave us unanswered, Diana, especially not someone who's sincerely and wholeheartedly waiting for news of her mother. God's greatness will not allow those He has created to remain uninformed of themselves or of God Himself. Some people believe God is too great and too exalted to involve Himself in our daily lives. On the contrary, it's because He is so great and exalted that He is involved in even the least of our affairs."

Zeynep Hanim's eyes shone. "He does concern Himself with us, Diana, He does. And in the best way. He takes an interest in Diana, in Maria, in Zeynep. In each of us, personally and individually. He is always with us, but to realize this, we, too, have to be with Him. Maria felt God was always taking care of her, that's why she asked Him about her mother."

"I also asked," Diana said. "I prayed to God so many times for news of my mother. I pleaded with Him, but I never received a reply. I'm sorry, but God does leave us unanswered."

"No, He doesn't. But He may send the answers in unexpected ways. Sometimes through a dream, sometimes a rose, perhaps a mother or even a beggar."

"A beggar?!"

"Did I say something wrong, my dear?"

Diana didn't know what to say. She wanted to believe that what Zeynep Hanim had said was only a coincidence. Trying to hide her astonishment, she gestured that Zeynep Hanim should continue.

"Just like you, Diana, Maria hasn't heard any news of her mother yet. But she certainly will. And not the news that she lost her mother but the news that she'll never lose her."

"And how will that happen?" Diana asked, her voice breaking.

"If God so wishes, anything can happen. If God so wills, just to send Maria news of her mother, sixty-seven years ago, a man and a woman fall in love. They get married, and two years later, a daughter is born to them. Even though the doctor says this premature infant can't live, the baby survives and flourishes... Many years later, as a grown woman, in the course of one of her journeys to far-off countries, she meets an old gardener. This gardener tells her that he can teach her how to hear roses. She believes him and for the next twenty years, she dedicates herself to the art of hearing roses. During this time, she goes through many difficulties. Solely on account of this 'madness' of hers, her husband leaves her, she is rejected by the people around her and is left with no choice but to move away from her hometown, finally coming to Istanbul. Here, she buys a house with a garden and spends all her time with her roses. Within a short while, the seeds sown in her heart by the old gardener put forth shoots, and finally she is able to hear roses.

"Do you know why all these events and the many others going on around them occur, Diana? Perhaps simply because God wishes to make Maria hear her mother's voice through a rose. It's for this reason, a Zeynep is born, a garden is created and a rose blooms..."

Although Diana thought Zeynep Hanim was speaking with such certitude, since what she said was all based on the assumption that Maria could hear her mother's voice, Zeynep Hanim's words fell short of consoling her.

"Very well," Zeynep Hanim said. "That will do both for mathematics and as an introduction. I've talked myself hoarse, let's have a break, and we'll meet back here in thirty-three minutes, okay?"

"All right," Diana said. "But first, I have a question: What song were the roses singing?"

"I can't tell you that," Zeynep Hanim said. "If I did, you wouldn't strive to hear them yourself."

29

When they returned to their stools, Zeynep Hanim said, "Now, Diana, I'd like you to go to that fountain over there, wash your head thoroughly, and then come back here."

"But I washed my hair just this morning."

"I can see that, dear. Now please go and wash your head."

Shrugging her shoulders, Diana walked across to the fountain. The water was ice-cold and she couldn't help splashing her clothes. As she shivered in the early morning coolness, she felt glad she hadn't come there in winter. After wringing the water out of her hair and combing it through with her fingers, she returned to her stool like an obedient schoolgirl.

"Now, Diana, I'd like you to go to that fountain over there, wash your head thoroughly, and then come back here."

For a minute Diana felt as though she were experiencing a déjà vu. It wasn't just that the words which had been repeated but that the expression on Zeynep Hanim's face was also the same as before. Diana sat glued to her seat for a minute without saying a word.

Unable to resist the stern look in Zeynep Hanim's eyes, she went back to the fountain and washed her head again. As she headed back to her stool, she feared the possibility that Zeynep Hanim might again ask her to do the same thing.

"There you go," Zeynep Hanim said. "Now that's done, we can begin. Oh, before I forget, if this lesson goes well, I have a surprise for you in the next one."

"What kind of surprise?"

"Didn't I say it was a surprise?"

"I see... By the way, am I allowed to ask questions in the garden?"

"Of course you are. Only I should tell you that you don't need to understand the reason behind everything we do in the garden to achieve your goal. If you don't forget what you experience here, sooner or later, all your questions will be answered.

"During our time in the garden, you're both the student and the teacher. You already have all the answers. As I said earlier, at one time you even had the ability to hear roses. I'm just here to remind you of the things you've forgotten, that's all. Hearing roses is easy. Very easy. All you have to do is either recall what you've forgotten, or forget all you've been taught."

"But I still want to know why my hair had to be wet!"

"Every question in the garden is like a seed, Diana. In time, it grows roots, stems and buds and finally blossoms. I can assure you, you'll never forget for the rest of your life that one cool morning you had to wash your already clean hair twice. Once something is lived it can never be like it was not lived. And 'having lived it' will sooner or later give you the answer you've been looking for. But this time, let me answer your question for you... I wanted you to wash your head because that head belonged to Diana."

"But I *am* Diana!"

"Didn't we agree to wipe out the résumé?"

"Well, why did I have to wash it the second time then?"

"After the first time you were freed of Diana's hairstyle. But the mind which gave your hair that shape was still there."

"Oh, so by washing it the second time, I stopped thinking like Diana, is that it?" she asked with a skeptical smile. "I don't mean to judge, but all this sounds too formalistic."

"You're right; you can't cleanse the mind with water from a fountain. But it's a symbol. Silent at the moment, but if you don't disregard it, one day it'll speak to you. A print placed in your heart. It may not be apparent now, but when the right time comes, it'll be manifest."

"When is the right time?"

"Perhaps the day you finally realize that the things you know can no longer help you. Or perhaps when you realize that awareness is like a ladder and in order to climb higher, you shouldn't go back to the steps you've left behind."

Diana, anxious to see the garden, refrained from asking any more questions.

30

In spite of bending her head, Diana still hit it on the lintel of the door. But at least there really was a garden on the other side.

A thin mist, pearly pink in the early morning light, covered everything, giving the garden an air of mystery, yet still unable to conceal its rainbow colors. A narrow path of hexagon tiles wound its way among the roses. The light breeze made the roses sway in harmony with the nightingales flying above. Only the sound of the birds and the gentle murmur of the water in the marble pool broke the silence.

Diana stood for a moment with her eyes half shut, inhaling the perfume in the air. With each breath, she felt as if she was being drawn closer to some heavenly place. But she returned to reality as Zeynep Hanim took off her shoes and started to rub her bare feet in the earth.

"Come, dear," Zeynep Hanim said, "you do the same."

Assuming the same manner she'd had when going to the fountain, Diana took off her shoes and did as she was told.

"I know, asking this won't make any difference, but I still want to know why I now have a pair of dirty feet."

"The roses are always wary lest the beauty of a gift should make them forget the giver."

"Of course!" Diana said. "Why didn't I think of that?!"

"Roses never, not even for a moment, forget that their existence and beauty are gifts from the earth. They are well aware that when their time comes, they'll fade and fall to the earth as seeds, and that the earth will only accept the seeds of the roses which haven't forgotten where they've come from. By touching the earth with our bare feet, we show the roses that we haven't forgotten the earth, either. Roses appreciate this."

Zeynep Hanim put her sandals back on.

"Everything we've talked about so far has only been a preparation for the journey of hearing roses. Up till now, all has been about us, the seekers. But in the garden, the seeker must no longer exist but become completely absorbed in the roses. We must give them all we have, our minds, our hearts, our souls, everything. So Diana, if you're ready, we can begin."

Diana nodded.

"Very well then... What do you know about roses?" Zeynep Hanim asked.

"Nothing, from the way you see them, absolutely nothing."

"Excellent. That's always the best start. So now I can tell you the golden rule for hearing roses."

"Golden rule?"

"The golden rule says: Know thy rose."

Zeynep Hanim delicately caressed the petals of the orange rose on her left before continuing, "One can only learn about a rose from a rose. That's the only way to truly know her."

They began to walk toward the center of the garden. After a while, Zeynep Hanim stopped suddenly and bent down toward the yellow rose in front of her. "What's the matter, Yellow Flower? I've never seen you cry before. Why are you weeping in the garden of happiness?"

Diana watched Zeynep Hanim closely. The rose didn't utter a sound, but Zeynep Hanim seemed to listen to it intently, nodding her head from time to time as if in agreement.

"I'm so sorry, I had no idea, Yellow Flower," she said to the rose. "If our guest agrees, I'd like to hear your story from the beginning."

Zeynep Hanim turned to Diana. "Yellow Flower is very sad today. Would you mind staying for a little while and listening to what she has to say?"

"What do you mean? You know I can't hear it."

"I'll tell you what Yellow Flower is saying as she tells me her story."

"Well, I'll feel a bit strange, but okay."

Diana sat down on the ground where Zeynep Hanim pointed, tucking her legs underneath her. What did she care if her white pants got dirty if by sitting there she could offer some emotional comfort to a rose!

Zeynep Hanim turned to the rose. "She's Diana, Maria's twin."

"Glad to meet you, Diana," Yellow Flower said, speaking through Zeynep Hanim. "I'd have thought she was Maria herself if the little nightingale hadn't told me otherwise."

"Glad to meet you, too," Diana said, as if talking to herself.

"Well, Yellow Flower," Zeynep Hanim said, "tell us what's making you so sad."

"I'm so sorry," Yellow Flower said. "I know you're used to seeing roses happy in this garden, but today is the anniversary of the day my old friend Venus lost her scent. I get like this once a year, forgive me..."

"There's nothing to forgive, Yellow Flower," Zeynep Hanim said. "Sometimes happiness expresses itself best through the tears shed for a friend... But tell us, how did this happen? I would never have thought that a friend of yours could lose her scent."

"Well," Yellow Flower said. "Let me begin by telling you about the first scented rose, the one from which our kind originated, since this is closely related to the tragedy Venus lived through...

"One day, the Sultan of our kingdom wished to create a rose which would carry his own special scent. So he sprinkled the soil of his garden with the royal perfume. Later, he watered the garden with the elixir of life, so that his rose would never fade. And when it finally bloomed, he called it, 'The Rose of Nothingness.' Our Sultan chose this name deliberately, so that his rose would never forget it had no scent independent of the Sultan's perfume. Because where I come from, a rose is a rose only because of its scent.

"Some time later, the Sultan willed his perfume to be known by all his people, so he allowed his rose to be planted outside the imperial gardens. His rose, no longer watered with the elixir of life, would one day fade, but in time, its offspring would carry the Sultan's perfume to every corner of the kingdom.

"Venus and I were both its descendants, and we were planted in a small village square. We bloomed for the sole purpose of making the Sultan's perfume known to everyone, and thus, we wished to be loved only for the royal perfume we carried.

"There were two kinds of people living in our village: 'Those-like-Maria' and 'Others.' Those-like-Maria were the ones who could recognize we carried the Sultan's perfume, and so they were more interested in our scent than in anything else. Unlike them, Others only gave importance to our color, our stems, our petals, anything that is visible to the eye…

"One day, a merchant arrived in the village to sell artificial roses. Fake, lifeless, scentless roses... We could never have imagined that anyone would be interested in them. But within a short time, Others began to whisper: 'That merchant has such pretty roses. Their petals are of silky cloth, their colors never fade, and best of all, their stems have no thorns.'

"Before long, the merchant sold so many 'roses' that our village soon turned into a village of artificial roses. Those-like-Maria couldn't bear this and gradually left the village. And in the end, Venus and I were left with two things: A need to be loved and Others.

"At that time, we couldn't foresee the disaster this situation would lead us to. Soon after Those-like-Maria had all gone, little by little, we began to metamorphose into what Others valued in the hope of earning their love. And because it was only our external features that they valued, we became more and more concerned with our looks. We strove to stand up straight like the artificial roses; we tried to extend the time our leaves stayed on us. We didn't even weep during emotional times so our petals wouldn't become wrinkled. And soon, out of neglect, our scent started to fade away.

"We fashioned ourselves to meet the expectations of Others, taking one shape after another. We re-toned our colors, one tone after another. Others said, 'Grow higher,' so we grew higher. They said, 'Orient yourselves to this direction and to that,' so we did in a silent rush. First they were shaping us the way they liked, and then showering praises on us.

"But, in spite of all this, deep inside we felt we weren't loved. Only those who were interested in our scent could really love us. Because it is its scent which makes a rose a rose. The feeling Others had for us could only be admiration at best.

"I was conscious of all this, but Venus behaved as though she was unaware of the situation. I tried to warn her. I told her that Others were like an invisible worm which had found out our bed of crimson joy, destroying our lives. I said to her, 'We must immediately escape from here to a place where 'Those-like-Maria' live.' But she paid no heed to my words. 'You're not normal,' she said. I couldn't blame her for saying that; she was right. There were so many artificial roses in our village by then, that a rose had to be scentless to be normal.

"As I was trying to convince her, a swarm of ants appeared on the ground beside us. They formed themselves into these words: 'Object to Others.' Venus glanced at them scornfully and muttered, 'Damned ants, they're all over the place!'

"In the end, I realized I wouldn't be able to help Venus, so I decided at least to take care of myself. I had to leave the village as soon as possible, but I had no idea how to go about it. Roses have no feet, you know. So, I began to wait for someone to come along who'd uproot me and take me away.

"At last, they came: A bulky man, a thin child and a gray donkey. Although both the man and the child seemed quite exhausted, they weren't riding on the donkey but walking by its side. It was so odd, I couldn't make anything of the situation.

"They sank thankfully to the ground under a nearby tree. The boy turned to his father. 'Dad, I'm so exhausted, we almost died along the way. Where did we go wrong?'

'Shut your mouth,' the father said, giving the boy a cuff on the ear. 'Traveling on foot is always like that.'

'But we have a donkey, Dad! And a strong one, too.'

'Shut up, I said! Didn't you hear what people said when we were both riding on the donkey? Didn't they say, 'See those heartless brutes, two people on one poor donkey!' Heaven knows what others will think of me if they hear this in the village.'

'Yes, that's when you told me to get off. But, Dad, at least you were comfortable.'

'But then, I heard someone else saying, 'Look at that cruel man! He's riding on the donkey like a king while his poor child can barely walk.' I know that man. He's a real blabbermouth. Heaven knows what others will think of me if they hear this in the village.'

'Well, Dad, that's when you got off the donkey and put me on its back, instead. But, at least I was comfortable.'

'And later? What did people say? 'See that disrespectful boy, sitting there on the donkey when his poor father can only drag himself along.' I won't have anyone saying a child of mine doesn't respect his father. Heaven knows what others will think of me if they hear this in the village.'

'But, Dad! Then we were both left to walk!'

'Be quiet, foolish boy. At least no one can speak badly about us now.'

"Right then, a man nearby turned to his friend, saying, 'See those fools! They have a donkey, but they walked the whole way to the village on foot!'

"Hearing this, the father flushed red to the roots of his hair. The boy was smiling. It seemed he'd understood what his father had not. Indeed, children do understand.

"To attract the child's attention," Yellow Flower continued, "I used all my strength to release the remainder of my scent. As soon as the royal perfume reached him, the child turned to me. Because children always love the Sultan's perfume.

"When darkness fell, he tenderly uprooted me and placed me on the donkey's back.

"Before leaving, Venus spoke to me one last time. 'Yellow Flower,' she said. 'You say you're leaving to preserve your scent, but I see that it all faded away long ago.' The moment she said that, a tear trickled down my petals as I realized Venus had completely lost her scent. Because a rose is a mirror to another rose; when one looks at the other, she either sees her own scent or lack of it.

"The next morning when the boy's father noticed me, he warned his son not to load the donkey with 'useless things.' He then took me to the market and sold me. After traveling in the hands of many, I was finally brought by a rose-lover to your garden to reclaim my scent. I've been so happy here, but I can't help thinking about Venus on every anniversary of our parting."

There was a short silence.

"If she's finished telling her story," Diana said. "There's a question I'd like to ask Yellow Flower."

"Go ahead, my dear," Zeynep Hanim said.

"Yellow Flower, real roses like yourself must be bothered by the existence of artificial roses, isn't that so?"

"Why should we be?" Yellow Flower said. "Artificial roses exist only because there are real roses. Their existence only shows our value. Who would make an imitation of something which isn't valuable?"

Diana nodded.

"I'd like to ask you something, too," she said turning to Zeynep Hanim. "When Yellow Flower was talking about the father and the boy, it seemed like a story I'd heard before. If I'm not mistaken, a long time ago, my mother might have told me a similar story. Is that possible?"

"Why not?" Zeynep Hanim said. "The experience Yellow Flower had with the father and the boy is known as a Nasreddin Hodja story here. But our Hodja doesn't resemble the father Yellow Flower encountered at all. Hodja is much kinder and more loving."

Diana, puzzled, looked at Zeynep Hanim as if she was waiting for an explanation.

"Why are you so surprised, my dear? Nasreddin Hodja was also a gardener and naturally his stories were inspired by the roses."

Zeynep Hanim got up. "So, Diana. That's all for today. Tomorrow's lesson will begin at 5:57 am."

31

The next morning, Diana was up early again, though still feeling sleepy. Reflections on her first lesson had kept her awake until very late. Her mind was full of thoughts about Zeynep Hanim, the garden, Yellow Flower's story, the mathematics of hearing roses...

Diana felt a little overwhelmed by these thoughts. Yet, at the same time, she was somewhat consoled by the equation she'd learned in the mathematics of hearing roses.

The equation was applicable to any question which had an innumerable number of possible answers and which couldn't be answered by the five senses. Therefore, the answer to the question of what had happened to her mother could only be as correct as the answer to "What song are the roses singing?" Thus, the chance of her knowing what had happened to her mother was zero—or at least a "special zero." So it wasn't correct for her to decide that her mother didn't exist anymore. She was glad that her first lesson had at least helped her to realize this.

Putting on a red shirt and a pair of blue jeans, she hurried to get ready in time for her second lesson. At least today she didn't have to bother with her hair.

Realizing she was about to be late, Diana ran down the stairs to get to her stool by 5:57. When she arrived, she saw that Zeynep Hanim was already waiting there.

"Good morning, Diana. May I ask what time it is?"

Diana was somewhat relieved to see that the hand on her watch was only one minute past the scheduled time.

"Oh, good morning. It's 5:58."

"I thought so. Our lesson for today is over."

She's got to be kidding!

"Forgive me," Diana said. "You did warn me. I know I shouldn't have been late, not even by a minute, but—"

"There's nothing to forgive, dear. I already know how to hear roses. This time was for you. We'll postpone the lesson to tomorrow evening at 6:19."

"You can't be serious!"

Zeynep Hanim didn't respond.

"I can't believe this. I get up at 5:30 in the morning, do nothing to my hair just as you'd wish, get ready at lightning speed and rush down here. And believe it or not, I was even looking forward to the lesson. But now you tell me it is cancelled just because I'm one minute late."

Zeynep Hanim took Diana gently by the hand and led her to the entrance of the garden. With a wide sweep of her hand, she embraced the whole garden. "Look at the dozens of rose bushes, Diana, hundreds of roses and rose buds. Rose scent everywhere, more than the air itself... Isn't it a magnificent sight?"

"I agree, with all my heart, but I don't quite understand what you're trying to—"

"It can take only a minute to spread the seeds which make a garden. You know, even the longest dreams we have take less than a minute. Perhaps, they're trying to tell us that we don't have to spend a lifetime to realize our dreams. What they certainly do tell us, however, is the power every minute holds. You'll never be able to regain the minute you've just missed. Who knows, maybe this minute which connected 5.56 to 5.58 on May 21st was the very minute you'd hear a rose."

As Diana walked back to her room, she thought that perhaps the lesson had not been postponed after all.

32

Diana wasn't bored by being confined to the guesthouse for a day and a half; her mind was preoccupied with her twin. Maria had told Zeynep Hanim that she would be arriving within that week, so Diana should be meeting her very soon, perhaps today or tomorrow, or at the most, within a few days.

Her time in the garden, and especially the things Yellow Flower had said, forced Diana to think deeply about herself and Maria. This was making the meeting with her twin harder rather than easier; however, in spite of that, she was impatient to meet Maria.

As usual, Zeynep Hanim arrived right on the minute.

"How are you this evening, my dear? We can go straight into the garden, you must be keen to find out about the surprise I promised you in our first lesson."

When they'd strolled a little way into the garden, Zeynep Hanim stopped before a peach-colored rose. "Oh, no, this isn't her."

After walking a few steps away from the rose, she turned to Diana. "She wanted to know if you were Maria."

"It seems as if everything in this garden revolves around Maria," Diana said. "I was going to ask you yesterday when we were with Yellow Flower, but it slipped my mind. How can the roses recognize someone who came to your garden so many years ago?"

"Even though a rose blossom lasts for only a few weeks at the most, many of the rose bushes you see in this garden were here when Maria came. She made such a great impression on them that they all said Maria was like water. In the language of roses, to say someone is 'like water' is the highest compliment a rose can pay. That's because roses are also like water; what they are inside is what they are on the outside. And they expect the same from us. The roses felt that Maria could fulfill this expectation in every way.

"They wanted me to tell Maria what a unique person she was. When I told her this, she blushed scarlet, and in reply she said, 'If there's anything unique about me, it's only because of my love for the roses.' The fact that Maria defined her self-worth only by the love she had for the roses pleased them very much and so they wished their voices to be heard by her. But at the time, that wasn't possible. First, Maria had to reach a certain level of maturity.

"The roses were quite sure that one day, she'd return to the garden to hear the roses which would bloom generations after them. They held a meeting and came to a unanimous decision that each rose, before it faded, would pass on what it knew about Maria to the young rose buds which would bloom after it. In turn, those rose buds would pass on the information to the next generation which would then pass it on to the following one, and so on. So in this way, all the qualities known about Maria were transmitted from one flowering to the next for many years. From that day on, every rose which has bloomed in this garden has hoped to be among the 'fortunate generation' of roses which would speak with Maria.

"Moreover, at this meeting, another important decision was made: It would be made possible for Maria to hear the rose called Socrates."

"Socrates?"

"He is the most precious rose in the garden and the last step in the art of hearing roses. He speaks only through poems. Maria didn't meet Socrates when she was here; she just wasn't ready for it. But ever since, the roses of this garden have been living with the hope of witnessing the celebrated meeting of Socrates and Maria."

Diana felt as if she was listening to some kind of fairytale. The real and the unreal were so intermingled in her mind that she no longer knew what to think or feel. But at least she now knew who the Socrates in Maria's third letter was.

Diana's eyes searched the rose garden looking for a rose which stood out. But she was unable to see any rose that was more beautiful or in any way different from the others.

"Is it possible for us to see Socrates?" Diana asked.

"If you really want to see him, you certainly can. In fact, that was my surprise for you. Follow me."

After a few minutes, they almost reached the end of the garden leaving the farthest rose bushes behind. Zeynep Hanim stopped as they came to a bare patch of earth about a meter square.

"Here we are," Zeynep Hanim said.

Pretty much every inch of the garden was densely planted with rose bushes. Except for this patch! Diana waited in silence as Zeynep Hanim stood there motionless.

After a while, Diana could contain herself no longer and burst out. "Why are we standing here like this? I thought we were going to see Socrates."

"We're right beside him. Socrates is standing right in front of you in all his glory!"

"You're joking, right? Please tell me you're joking."

Zeynep Hanim cupped her hand in the air as if she were holding a rose-blossom in it. "Just look at the beauty of this rose."

But no sooner had she said it than she shook her head regretfully. "I'm so sorry, Diana, I shouldn't have mentioned to you the beauty of something you can't see."

As Diana stared at her in astonishment, Zeynep Hanim asked, "You don't really believe Socrates is standing right in front of you, do you?"

"Well, it's a little difficult for me to believe that."

"In that case, let me just ask you this," Zeynep Hanim said. "Why is it that for years others have managed to make you believe you can't hear a rose, but I can't make you believe for even a second that you can't see a rose?"

Without waiting for an answer, she pointed to the open patch. "A week ago, Socrates was planted in this very spot. I wanted to give him to Maria as a present so I sent him to a friend of mine, a nurseryman, for the necessary preparations."

"Oh, I see," Diana said. "Well, I really needed an explanation. What a surprise! I nearly ran away from here."

"I owe you an apology, my dear," Zeynep Hanim said. "There's no such thing as a white lie... A lie is a lie. However, if a lie helps us to see a much bigger one, say for example, the lie that we can't hear roses, I guess it could be forgiven. But I still offer you my apologies and hope you'll forgive me for the sake of my intention."

Diana smiled. "That's okay."

When they reached the door, Zeynep Hanim said, "Why don't we postpone tomorrow morning's lesson to 15:31. But wait for me in your room at around half-past nine tomorrow morning. Perhaps we'll take a cruise along the Bosphorus, what do you think?"

"Oh, that would be wonderful!"

33

After returning from a splendid tour of the Bosphorus, Diana had gone to her room for a short rest before it was time for her lesson. Her mind was still on the day she'd spent in Zeynep Hanim's company.

Fetching Diana from her room in the morning, Zeynep Hanim had driven her to a small neighborhood on the shore called Ortakoy. After eating Shazeli Kebab in a small restaurant there, they'd boarded a private boat and set off from the quay in front of the ornate stone-built mosque.

On the calm blue waters of the Bosphorus, they'd sailed along the European coast up as far as Rumeli Fortress. Then, the boat crossed to the Asian side and made its way downstream toward the Sea of Marmara. At its entrance, they'd had lunch on a tiny island where stood the Maiden's Tower, which had only recently been reopened to the public after being closed for centuries. Diana had thought the kebab had been filling enough for lunch, but then she'd been unable to resist the tempting dishes of Ottoman cuisine served one after the other.

Zeynep Hanim had forbidden any talk on the subject of roses or of Maria until their lesson. Instead, they'd laughed a lot, even engaging in a joke-telling competition.

Diana thought that Zeynep Hanim had taken every care to make the day memorable. She'd felt so pampered that she hadn't been able to help wondering whether Zeynep Hanim hadn't mistaken her for Maria again.

As she was going down to the garden for her lesson, she wondered whether the laughter which had been on Zeynep Hanim's face all day would be replaced by an expression more in keeping with the seriousness of 'the art of hearing roses.'

At exactly the appointed minute, she heard Zeynep Hanim's voice: "Let's go straight into the garden, dear. Come, let's not waste any time."

Diana followed Zeynep Hanim as she strode with hasty steps along the garden path. When they reached the center of the garden, Diana noticed at the side of the path a large pot she hadn't seen there before. In it, were two separate roses, their stems entwined like climbing roses. One of them was red, the other white.

The blossom of the red rose stood up straight while that of the white one faced the ground. So closely were their stems and leaves interlocked, one might have thought that in the pot there was only one rose with flowers of two different colors.

"Is this Socrates?" Diana asked.

"No, its name is written on the pot."

Diana bent down to look at the name, "Ephesus" was written there in tiny letters.

"Ephesus... The ancient city?"

"Exactly. Once built where Selcuk is now, in the west of Turkey."

"Did the pot come from there? I can't see any other roses in pots, are you going to plant these two roses in the garden, too?"

"Yes, the pot did come from Ephesus. We've kept it inside since then, but last night we brought it out. Whether we'll plant the Rose of Ephesus here or not is solely dependent on these two roses. They have three days. They'll either be planted in the garden or be sent back to Ephesus; this will be decided by the test they'll be put through."

Having long since learned not to be surprised at the things Zeynep Hanim said, "What kind of a test?" was all Diana asked, as though it was the most natural thing for roses to undergo a test before being planted.

"One of the most important qualities of the roses in this garden is their ability to live in harmony with one another, regardless of their differences in color, size, or origin. Their life here is free of dispute, jealousy, or vanity. So whenever we plant a new rose, we have to be very selective and careful. Roses are influenced by each other and, in time, take on the state of the roses around them. We have a wonderful proverb for this: 'Grapes grow black by looking at each other.' That's why before we plant a rose, we want to know whether or not it will have a negative effect on the other roses.

"Besides, the case of Ephesus is particularly special. This two-headed rose took on this shape after two roses with totally different characteristics were planted in the same pot. In time, their roots have become so entangled that it's no longer possible to separate them. What makes them so unusual is they are constantly in conflict. For us to plant them in the garden, first they have to prove to us that they can manage to be 'one rose.'"

After looking thoughtfully at Ephesus, Zeynep Hanim continued, "But this won't be that easy, I'm afraid. Although they both come from the same region and the same soil, the way each regards herself is very different. The red rose used to be planted at the temple of Artemis in Ephesus and the white one at the house of Santa Maria, also in Ephesus. The red one believes she's Artemis, the goddess of the hunt, and refuses to answer to any other name. The white one has no preference in this matter, but we call her Miriam."

"Did you just say 'goddess of the hunt'?" asked Diana. "Wasn't Diana the goddess of the hunt? Because I have her name, my friends sometimes call me 'goddess'..."

"True, in Roman mythology, Diana *is* the goddess of the hunt. But she's known as Artemis in Greek mythology. The myths about Artemis date further back, and she underwent some changes before she became known as 'Diana,' in Latin scriptures."

After remaining silent for a while, Diana asked, "What kind of conflict are these roses involved in?"

"Would you like me to relay their conversation to you?"

Even though Diana wished to mask it from Zeynep Hanim, she really wanted to hear the dialogue between Artemis and Miriam.

"Why not," she said. "If it won't interfere with our lesson…"

Zeynep Hanim sat on the ground next to the pot. Diana did the same.

"Hello, Ephesus," Zeynep Hanim said, "is it okay if we listen to you for a little while?"

After a few seconds, she turned to Diana. "Artemis scolded me, saying, 'My name is Artemis, not Ephesus, you old lady!' Since that's what she wants, I'll address the Rose of Ephesus by using their individual names. I'll repeat their conversation to you word for word. Are you ready?"

Diana nodded her head, and so Zeynep Hanim began to relay the dialogue between Artemis and Miriam:

"Couldn't you be more polite, Artemis?" Miriam said. "It shouldn't really matter what name we're called by."

"What do you mean 'it shouldn't matter'" Artemis said. "I have a name. A great name which is on every tongue, a name praised to the skies. I am Ar-te-mis! My name is renowned everywhere and gods know me well. I am the high and exalted Artemis, I am the most beautiful of all the beautiful. I am a goddess, not just a flower like you. The most flowers can be are ornaments in my temple. "

"Have you noticed something?" Miriam asked.

"What?"

"All you say is 'I,' 'me,' 'my.'"

"Of course I will say 'I' 'me' 'my!' If Artemis doesn't deserve to say 'I', who does? A mortal flower like you?"

"You always say the same thing, you're a goddess and I'm just a flower. But you know what the truth is."

"What truth?"

"Oh, never mind. I don't want to upset you."

"You? You upset me? Don't make me laugh, you poor flower. A flower will upset Artemis? Hah hah haaah!... You go ahead, funny flower, please try to upset me."

"Fine, Artemis, but first tell us who Artemis really is. Tell us so that the whole garden can know."

"Oh, what nonsense! Who wouldn't know Artemis? Who wouldn't know me?"

"We're not in your temple, Artemis. This is a rose garden. The roses may not know who you are. Is it not their right to know who the exalted Artemis is? You're the greatest! So please honor us by telling us about yourself."

"For once, you've spoken the truth, flower. Yes, everyone has the right to hear of my greatness, and roses, too, should know how great Artemis is. So be silent and listen…

"I!.. I am Artemis, daughter of Zeus, god of gods. I used to live in Ephesus, the city known for my temple, not for Santa Maria's dilapidated old cottage. For hundreds of years, I received those who came to worship me in my temple, which is one of the Seven Wonders of the World, by the way. Thousands of people, thronging like ants, came from afar just for me. In masses they came. To praise me, exalt me and bow down before me, trampling on one another in their eagerness.

"Do you understand, you worthless flower; do you see the greatness of Artemis now? Those people who pick flowers like you to thrust into vases came to my threshold like slaves.

"Hey you, roses of the garden, do you hear me? Now you, too, know the greatness of Artemis, don't you?"

"You've said exactly what I expected you'd say," Miriam said. "When I asked you to tell us about yourself, you started by telling us about your father, the splendor of your home, and those who praised you. But I didn't ask for any of that. All I asked was who *you* were."

"You poor, miserable flower, what are you trying to say? If you want to know who I am, then know that I am Greatness. *That's* who I am."

"What makes you believe you're so great?"

"If I weren't great, would thousands of people be interested in me? Would they praise me till their tongues stick to the roof of their mouths? Would they be enslaved by me?"

"The truth is," Miriam said, "you're the one who's enslaved by them. But you just don't want to see it."

"Oh, you're so jealous, you don't know what you're saying."

"It's true, you are indeed their slave. Who is Artemis, really? Nothing but an illusion, shaped and worshipped by Others. Who created Artemis? Wasn't it those humans you so despise, who first created in their minds an image of beauty to worship and then shaped you into this figure by their praises? Don't be deceived by their later becoming passionately devoted to you. It was they who invented you, they who determined your qualities, and they who exalted your name. I'm sorry, but you don't have an independent existence of your own. You only exist by them. You exist by their praise, their adoration, their applause. You're dependent on Others."

"Now you've gone too far, you flower! First look at yourself before you speak. Who do you think you are to talk to me like this, you little thing?"

"Yes, you're right. I'm nothing great. But I'm a rose... I'm a rose whether I'm admired or not, whether anyone's crazy about me or not. Like I said, nothing great. Just a rose... But, do you know what it means to be a rose, my friend? Being a rose means 'freedom.' It means not existing by the praises of Others or not ceasing to exist by their disapproval. Don't get me wrong; I, too, love people. I want them to visit me and smell my scent. But I only want this so I can offer them my perfume.

"True, maybe I've never had as many visitors as you. Maybe those who came to visit the house of Santa Maria failed to notice the little rose planted there. Yet still, there were a handful of people who did notice me. But never mistake these people for the kind who came to worship you."

"Of course not, how could I?" Artemis said. "My visitors came in thousands!"

"Do you remember how those who came flocking to you on sunny days, began, one by one, to desert you when autumn came? And in the depths of winter, there was no one at your side. Your pride only deepened your loneliness, and you couldn't even weep because of that empty pride of yours. The higher their praises had raised you in spring, the greater the fall you had to face in autumn. The change in the weather instantly knocked you down."

"Nonsense! That's just the way autumn is."

"Not for roses, Artemis. To a rose, autumn means rain. Autumn means a time to prepare for spring. And those who come for a rose are never as disloyal as those who came to worship you. Those who worship, worship only for themselves. Unlike your visitors, those who visited me came only for my scent. I never expected them to bow down before me. No, that wouldn't be love. Love doesn't lower the lovers, but raises them."

"Oh, you worthless flower, what can you ever understand about being adored?"

"I'm sorry, my friend, but those who are fervently devoted to you will desert you one day. Because it's not you they worship, but their own passions. A day will come when their passion will find another goddess. A more beautiful, more enticing, more desirable goddess! So you will be forgotten. And because you owe your existence to their praises, once you're forgotten, you'll cease to exist."

"No, I will live forever! You're the mortal one, remember?"

"True, I'm not immortal. One day I'll fade and return to the earth. I'll die, but my life will not end. Because that earth will nurture another rose. Apart from those who love me for my scent, no one will remember me. No one will think that a dead rose could still release her beautiful scent. But when my friends breathe the air which I'll be drifting in, a smile will shine on their faces. And so I'll be able to say, 'My life hasn't been in vain.' 'The darkness I had to live through before my rose blossomed wasn't for nothing,' I'll say. 'I'm glad I was content to be just a rose...'

"Come, my friend, may you, too, be content to be just a rose. Stop covering the truth. Reveal your rose face, and become one with me. Come, let's ask the gardener to break our pot. Don't you see, even the greatest pots are too small for real roses?"

"I'm *not* a rose, you stupid flower!" Artemis said. "I am a goddess!"

"If wearing that 'mask of greatness' is making you happy, don't take it off, keep on wearing it. Keep on saying 'me.'

But know there's a price to pay. Know that the price of saying 'me' all the time is to forget the real You..."

"You gardener! You old woman! Take this pathetic flower away from me!"

"As you know, my friend," Miriam said, "it's not possible for us to be separated ever again. Whether we like it or not, we have to live our whole life together. As long as we go on being two different voices speaking in the same pot, not only will we never find peace with each other, but we'll spoil the peace of the other roses, too. And even the peace within people... We'll flow into those who smell us as two conflicting voices. One minute you'll say one thing, the next minute I'll say something else, one minute Artemis, the next Miriam, and so it'll go on and on like this. Sometimes we'll both talk at once. As if the noise in our pot isn't enough, we'll carry our noise into people. But we have no right to make either them or ourselves unhappy."

"If that is so," Artemis said, "submit to my voice. Become me!"

"You know, I would if I could; I'd declare to the world that I was Artemis, just to be one voice with you. But I can't. Not just because I know I'm a rose, but because I know you're one, too. Maybe I could let go of myself, but I could never let go of you. Because it's by looking at you that I've come to know myself."

"That can't be true, I am Artemis and you're just a poor flower."

"Artemis, I've heard that they call you 'protector of the poor.' Also, that you use your arrow to offer a sudden, sweet death… Is that true?"

"Yes, indeed, it's all true."

"Well, if I am poor, then protect me. Protect me from yourself! Right now, at this very moment! Tighten your bow, draw your arrow, and give yourself a sudden, sweet death. Don't be afraid, you won't fade into nothingness. Artemis never had a real existence, so how can she ever cease to exist? But when your fancied self has tasted that sweet death, you'll be reborn. Reborn as a rose. I know, it's not easy, but I beg you to try.

"So, Artemis… Will you?"

Artemis didn't respond.

"Please," Miriam said. "You recall being a rose, right?"

Zeynep Hanim remained silent for a while. Then, she turned to Diana.

"Artemis refuses to reply to Miriam."

"Didn't she say anything?" asked Diana.

"Nothing," Zeynep Hanim said, getting to her feet. "I think that's enough for today, my dear. Tomorrow's lesson, our fourth and last, will start at one minute past four in the morning."

Diana felt as if every part of her, especially her mind, had gone numb. There were so many things she wanted to say, but she chose to remain silent.

34

Diana, in her white nightgown, stood outside the door of room Number 1. What would Zeynep Hanim's reaction be to an uninvited guest knocking on her door after midnight?

If only she could wait another three hours, in the garden she could ask Zeynep Hanim all the questions she wanted and wouldn't have to disturb her at this crazy hour. But she couldn't face the thought of tossing and turning in bed for all those hours.

She tapped gently on the door.

Zeynep Hanim opened the door in a matter of seconds. The first thing Diana noticed was Zeynep Hanim's white nightgown which was very similar to the one she herself was wearing. In fact, they were identical.

"I'm so sorry to disturb you. Maybe you'd gone to bed, maybe I'm violating your rules, but I just couldn't wait. I really need to talk to you. But I guess this isn't the right time..."

"It's one o'clock, my dear. I was just about to go to sleep. It's certainly not the time to come knocking on anyone's door, let alone on that of an old woman like me."

She was absolutely right. Diana couldn't blame her. She wished the floor would open and swallow her up.

"Please come in," Zeynep Hanim said.

"But you just said—"

"Do you think I don't realize how difficult it must have been for you to knock on my door at this time of night? But you did it. Because it was more difficult for you to sleep in a comfortable bed than to come here. In such a situation, one usually has something to say that's worth listening to. Come on in."

Diana, with her head bowed down, entered the dimly lit room.

They sat down facing each other by the window overlooking the garden.

"I don't know where to start..."

"Why don't you begin with the most difficult part, and the rest will follow."

"Maria," Diana said. "Maria and I... Maria... She's always on my mind. I can't stop myself from thinking about her... I know, there isn't much time left till we meet; who knows, perhaps tomorrow... But the things I've experienced here, in the garden..."

She paused for a moment, and then she continued:

"Until I met you, I'd forced myself to believe Maria was crazy. I'd put all other possibilities aside. After all, in her letters she mentioned speaking with roses... But I don't think that was the real reason why I completely shut myself off from her. She was the one who caused my mother to spend the last days of her life in worry and fear. Yet, besides all that, I felt something else as I was reading Maria's letters. Something I was afraid to admit even to myself; something I was afraid would destroy me..."

"What was it?"

"It was as if Maria was the person I'd always wanted to be but had failed to become. I couldn't help feeling that she was so like my mother..."

Diana heaved a sigh before going on. "There's nothing wrong with a daughter being like her mother, of course. But if the daughter who was separated from her mother at the age of one resembles her more than the twin sister who has lived with her twenty-four years longer, it's pretty hard for the twin to accept, especially when that twin lost her mother just as she was beginning to discover her. Especially if that twin hadn't had the chance to tell her mother even once how much she wanted to be like her..."

Diana's eyes filled with tears. Zeynep Hanim pulled her chair closer and took Diana's hands in hers.

"Don't worry, my dear, such a mother would already know what her daughter wished to say, even if she hadn't had the chance..."

"After coming here, I realized that what I'd resisted taking from my mother, Maria had taken from you. And that's the reason why I can't be like Maria."

"Why do you think you can't be like her?"

"My mother used to say, 'The only thing you need in order to feel special is yourself.' But I didn't want to understand this. I was always in need of something else: other people's attention, praise, anything which made me feel special…

"I wasn't someone who could live without being admired. I loved being the belle of the ball, I loved the Diana in the eyes of 'Others.' Maybe just because of that, I gave up my biggest dream of becoming a writer.

"It was as if Maria's first letter was describing me. The constant attention of the people around her, the fact that she wasn't happy in spite of that, and her almost giving up her biggest dream just because of Others..."

"You see, my dear, Maria went through the same things as you did. It isn't only you; to a certain extent, all of us give up something of ourselves in order to win the approval of the people around us."

"Yes, but in the end, Maria could manage to pursue her dream. Unlike me, she wasn't enslaved by the expectations of Others… In our first lesson, when we were listening to Yellow Flower, do you know what I thought? It was as though Yellow Flower was Maria and I was Venus... And later, Miriam and Artemis..."

Diana paused to see if Zeynep Hanim would show any reaction to the parallel she'd drawn between herself and Venus and Artemis. When she was sure that Zeynep Hanim's expression wouldn't change, she carried on: "I'm not saying this because Diana is another name for Artemis or because of the connection between the names Miriam and Maria. Believe me, I've learnt not to occupy my mind with coincidences I can't explain.

"But there's one thing I should occupy my mind with: the fact that, just like Artemis, I'm dependent on Others. And that in order to hide this, for years I've been walking around wearing the 'mask' of a goddess. Now I realize that in trying to become greater, I only became smaller... Am I wrong? Isn't what I'm saying about Maria and myself the truth?"

"Diana, you complain of Others' influence on you, but at the same time you're asking an 'other' person for her opinion. Don't forget, I'm also one of the Others."

"No, Zeynep Hanim. Maria said you were a Non-Other and I agree with her. Please, tell me the truth; I'm not mistaken in what I think about Maria and myself, am I?"

Zeynep Hanim looked at Diana, her eyes filled with compassion. "I think you're being too hard on yourself, Diana. None of us is perfect. Nor do we have to be. Everyone wishes to be admired and accepted by the people around them; it's quite normal."

"What if we live a life Others have chosen for us rather than the one we would choose for ourselves? Is this also normal?"

"My dear, neither I nor anyone else has the right to judge the way you live your life. Maybe I can teach you to hear roses, and on that subject, I can certainly give you a lot of advice. In the garden, I may tell you to do this or that for as long as you care to listen. That's because the art of hearing roses is something I know and you have little knowledge of. And you asked me to teach it to you. But don't ask me about yourself, Diana. I don't know you. And even if I did, I can never teach you about yourself.

"As far as Maria's concerned, really, I know much less about Maria than you think. I saw no more of her than I've seen of you. But from what I do know, I can say she's someone extremely courageous."

"And," she added, "As beautiful as you are."

Diana smiled gratefully at Zeynep Hanim.

I'm glad I knocked on the door, she thought. She didn't feel like going back to her room but wished she could stay and be with Zeynep Hanim all nightlong.

But what good would that do? Hadn't she stayed with her mother for twenty-five years?

"I think I should be going now," Diana said softly. "I don't know how to thank you for your time and for your kindness."

"I haven't done anything," Zeynep Hanim said. "But you're certainly right, my dear, you should have a little rest. The last lesson is the toughest of all."

35

It was pitch-dark. When Diana went down to the garden, there were still nineteen minutes until the time of the lesson. She'd come a little earlier this morning to spend some time alone with the roses before the lesson began.

As she was about to enter the garden, she suddenly heard footsteps approaching on the wooden floor of the house. They didn't seem at all like those of Zeynep Hanim; she'd always come exactly on time to the previous lessons, never a minute early or a minute late. Moreover, her footsteps were always steady and unhurried. But the approaching footsteps were fast and worried, their pace increasing constantly. From the tap-tapping sound they made, it seemed as if the person was almost running.

It was indeed Zeynep Hanim who came up to Diana panting, her face damp with perspiration.

"Oh, Diana," she said, her voice trembling, "I know you were really waiting for this, but—"

"What is it?! Is it, is it Maria?!"

Zeynep Hanim bowed her head.

"What's happened? Please tell me everything's all right."

"Maria called; I was asleep. But, thankfully, she left a message. She said something urgent had come up, and so she had to go to Rio."

"Oh, my God! She must have heard of my mother's illness. I must return home immediately, I must get home before her!"

"But Maria's already—"

"I hope she hasn't heard of Mom's death," Diana murmured.

What would learning of her mother's death do to a girl who had dedicated all her life to meeting her mother? Even the thought of it made Diana shiver. But at least Maria had said it was urgent. She wouldn't have been in such a hurry to see a grave, would she?

"I'm sorry, but I must go and pack right away."

"Of course, my dear. In the meantime, I'll reserve a seat for you on the first available flight."

As Diana was about to head back inside, she suddenly stopped. Turning round, she hurried toward the center of the garden and sank to her knees in front of Yellow Flower. She caressed her petals with her fingertips.

"You are right, Yellow Flower. It is its scent, above all, that makes a rose a rose."

36

A seat was found for Diana on the noon flight, and they arrived at the airport just in time. Before she got into the line for passport control, Diana hugged Zeynep Hanim.

"Thank you for everything you've done for me. I don't know how I can possibly ever repay you. The days I spent with you were perhaps the most extraordinary days of my life. If you'd ever met my mother you'd understand why I can only say 'perhaps.'"

"Thank yourself, Diana. What made this week special had nothing to do with me or with our unfinished lessons. What made it special was the courage with which you faced the roses. That's not something one person can give to another.

"You came here as an intelligent, well-educated person. But that didn't stop you from trying to listen to the roses. Trust me, this isn't as easy as one may think. Only those who have the courage to give up the good can reach the better. You have that courage."

Diana smiled. "I don't think I deserve such a compliment, but I'm so happy to have had the privilege of knowing you. I want you to know that I'm leaving my heart here. And I hope that one day I'll return to the rose garden to complete my unfinished lesson."

"We are wherever our heart is. If your heart is here, no matter how far away you are physically, the lesson will be completed; never doubt that."

Zeynep Hanim took a small bottle of perfume from her purse. "In the rush, I didn't have time to wrap this for you. It's a fragrance blended from the scents of the roses in the garden. There are one hundred different scents in it, including that of Socrates. The unique thing about this perfume is that it seems different each time you smell it. I'm sure it'll suit you perfectly."

"I don't know what to say. You can't imagine what this means to me. I'm so sorry, I have nothing to give you."

"You already have, my darling. Being my guest was the greatest gift you could possibly give me."

When it was time to say goodbye, for a moment, Diana saw her mother in Zeynep Hanim's deep blue eyes. Putting her bag down, she embraced her once more. "Oh, I can't believe it, you are so much like my mother..."

"One day, my darling," Zeynep Hanim whispered in her ear, "you, too, will hear the roses. When this happens, don't think of it as a miracle; that'd make you forget that every moment of life is a miracle. Always remember, not only roses, but everything speaks."

37

Full of apprehension, the passengers waited anxiously to hear the pilot announce that there was nothing to worry about. As the plane lurched sickeningly up and down, it seemed that at any moment the wings would break off. Everyone except Diana was alarmed by each eerie mechanical noise coming from the plane.

Diana was waiting impatiently for the "Fasten Your Seat Belts" sign to be switched off so she could reach into the overhead locker for her diary.

That sign's never going to go off...

She undid her seat belt and got to her feet, taking no notice of the stares of the other passengers or of the stewardess sitting at the back of the plane. At that instant, the plane shook again and she found herself on the lap of the passenger sitting next to her.

"Oh, I'm so sorry, sir."

"You could have hurt yourself, miss, you'd better sit down," the elderly man said.

The stewardess motioned to her, insisting she sit down, and some of the passengers turned around as if wondering what was the matter with her.

Straightening up, she reached deep into the overhead locker for her bag which bounced up and down ready at any moment to fall on top of another passenger. But she managed to seize it without any accident.

Opening her diary, Diana began to write with crooked letters in-between moments of turbulence:

My Beloved Mother,

I want to ask you something…

Maria was born before me, wasn't she? She learned to walk before me and talked before me, didn't she?

Unfortunately, she's still a step ahead of me now. Maybe, even as I write this, she's about to join you…

Actually, Mom, Maria deserved to be with you a long time ago. She certainly deserves you more than I did. She loves you like crazy.

Don't get me wrong, I love you, too. I love you as much as she does. But she loves you without ever knowing the sweetness of being your daughter. She loves you without receiving anything from you, or being sheltered in your arms when she was frightened, or falling asleep with her head cuddled against your chest. As you used to say, "Love is not love if the lover asks for something in return."

So, Mom... Which of us is more worthy to be your daughter? Maria or me? I'm not scared of the answer any more. She's my twin. Since I've always followed after her, maybe one day I'll deserve to be your daughter, too.

After all, haven't she and I shared the same destiny up to now? Growing up with only one parent, being surrounded by the attention of Others, our love for stories, our dreams, Zeynep Hanim and the rose garden... According to the order in which things happened to Maria, it should soon be my turn to speak with a rose... But right now, that doesn't seem very likely. A part of me still thinks that such things only happen in fairytales.

But there's still a question I can't get out of my mind, Mom... In fairytales, heroes never make promises they can't keep, isn't that so? In that case, if the things I've heard in the rose garden are part of a fairytale, doesn't that make Zeynep Hanim the heroine? So she has to keep her promise, doesn't she? "One day, you, too, will hear the roses," was what she said to me...

I don't know, Mom...

Fantasy-reality; fear-hope; me-Maria... How mixed-up everything's become.

I so badly need to hear your voice...

Diana

Your little daughter

38

As soon as she saw the hotel chauffeur who'd come to fetch her from the airport, Diana asked, "Has anyone come to the hotel asking for my mother? Someone who looks just like me?"

"Not as far as I know, Senhora Oliveira."

"Then let's quickly stop by the hotel before we go home."

Diana counted the minutes all the way to the hotel, until finally they arrived. But to her disappointment, she got the same answer from the hotel staff and, later, from the people who worked in the house: no one had been asking for her mother. Since for the time being Diana did not wish to tell anyone that she had a twin, she even tried asking, "Did anyone see me here last week?" As everyone knew she'd been away, no one took this question seriously.

The fact that Maria hadn't come either to the hotel or to the house could mean that she hadn't heard of her mother's death yet. This was good news. But Diana did not feel at peace as Maria could still have heard about it from another source.

There was nothing she could do but stay home and wait. She walked for hours up and down the house, listening for the doorbell or the telephone to ring. No one came and no one phoned...

This waiting continued until midnight when her exhausted body finally accepted defeat, and she fell asleep on the black sofa.

39

Startled by the doorbell, she woke up suddenly and ran to the door, reaching it before Senhora Lopez. It was the postman. Diana took the envelope he held out to her and shut the door. There was neither name nor return address on the envelope, but she had the feeling that it must have something to do with Maria. Hastily she ripped it open.

My Beloved Mother,

Today I arrived in Rio. They told me you were dead. I didn't believe it.

Mommy, where are you? Where have you gone, just as we were about to meet at last?

Oh, Mom, I miss you so terribly... You miss me, too, don't you?

So come and take me. I am at the address I wrote in my fourth letter.

I am sure you'll come because I know you're alive.

You must come.

Because if you don't, I'll have to accept that what Others told me all along was the truth. I will have to accept that I'll never meet you in this world.

And in that case, I will do what it takes and come to you myself.

Maria

"Oh, my God," whispered Diana. "There was no letter in the fourth envelope."

40

Diana phoned Zeynep Hanim to tell her about Maria's note. Then, she began to hunt for the missing letter in every corner of the house. But, although she searched the antique chest, her mother's room and the library, ransacking every possible hiding place, she couldn't find the letter anywhere.

Toward the evening the phone rang.

"Hello, Diana," Zeynep Hanim said. "Have you managed to find the letter?"

"No, I've looked everywhere. I'm about to go crazy."

"Don't worry. When Maria doesn't get a response from your mother, I'm sure she'll try to contact her again."

"I've asked everyone here and they say no one came either to the hotel or to the house. And I've no idea who could have told Maria of our mother's death. I'm so afraid she'll do something stupid."

"No, no, you mustn't think like that. At the very least, she'll call me when she doesn't hear from your mother, don't worry... Tomorrow I'm going to send you a package by express delivery. Open it, and if Maria comes, please give it to her. Maybe it'll be some consolation for her. But in the meantime, you go on searching for the letter, my dear."

"Maybe there isn't such a letter!"

"Didn't you say there was a fourth envelope? If there's an envelope, there has to be a letter."

41

Diana searched for the letter for two days nonstop, but this led to nothing. She even went to her mother's grave to ask where the letter might be, but she received no answer.

When she got home, she went into the library. After looking through the shelves filled with hundreds of thick books, she finally found "The Little Prince," which she'd often read as a child. She took it from where it was wedged between two bulky books. In the farewell letter Maria had left for her father, she wrote that she'd reread *The Little Prince* after many years. She'd mentioned how the book had completely changed. Was she right?

Dusting off the cover, Diana sat on the floor and opened the book.

One hour later, she'd finished reading it. Leaning back against the wall, she reflected for some time on how different the book had become. Then, she reached for her diary.

Dear Maria,

I've just finished reading "The Little Prince" again after many years. You're right, the book has changed completely!..

I think I'm also beginning to realize what it means "to be responsible for a rose."

But that doesn't mean I'll be able to be responsible for it. And that's where you and I differ, Maria. You managed to be responsible for your rose.

You realized long before I did, that your rose was missing and you did all you could to find it. You took care of your rose...

You know what I'm thinking, Maria? I wish our father had taken me with him instead and left you with Mom. I wish Mom had dedicated her life to you instead of me. You are the one who deserved our mother.

I've come to realize that Mom didn't entrust you to me, but rather she entrusted me to you. She knew I needed you.

And now I know it, too.

That's why you must come here, Maria. You must once again believe that we can meet Mom in this world. You must feel that she is with God and God is always with us.

Remember when you were little... Remember your reply to Others? When Others told you your mother was dead or that she was some place far away or that you could never be with her again in this world? Didn't you believe that there had to be another answer?

So what's happened to make you change your mind? Or is it because you, too, have become a grownup like me?

Well, Maria, I won't give up hope that you'll come and find me here. Because this is what my heart tells me:

"Long before you began to search for Maria, she'd already begun to search for you..."

Diana

42

Only a few minutes after Diana had closed her diary, there was a ring at the door. She ran to open it.

It was Gabriel. In his arms was an enormous package.

"Good morning, Diana, an express delivery for you from Istanbul. Whose heart did you steal there?"

"I hope I managed to steal someone's," she said thinking of Zeynep Hanim.

The package was so trussed and bound that it resembled a mummy. Along with it, Gabriel held out an envelope to her. Having dispatched him with a warm smile, Diana opened the envelope.

Dear Diana,

Inside this package you will find Socrates and, on his branch, a crown woven of white roses, like the one Maria wore in her dream. Maria believed she would hear her mother's voice only if she'd listened to Socrates first. I hope her wish will be fulfilled soon.

Also, Yellow Flower has something to ask you…

She has adapted an anecdote of Nasreddin Hodja for Maria. She wants you to read the following story to her when you two meet. After Maria hears Socrates' verses, she'll need a key which can only be found through this story.

The Key to the Treasure

One day Nasreddin Hodja lost the key to his treasure. Although he searched the street in front of his house and around the neighboring houses, as well as along the road to the village, he couldn't find it anywhere.

So he called on his neighbors to help him find the key. They also looked high and low and all around the village but to no avail. It was as if the ground had opened and swallowed it up. Fortunately, some time later, it occurred to one of the neighbors to ask the Hodja:

"Hodja, are you sure you dropped the key outside?"

"Oh, no," the Hodja said. "I dropped it inside, but to search outside is easier, that's why I'm searching out here."

Yellow Flower says that Maria shouldn't search for the key to her treasure outside, but rather she should search for it inside...

And perhaps, in the drawer at the head of her bed.

Yellow Flower and I both want to thank you for all your help, my darling.

Zeynep

43

After Diana had cut through the strong styrofoam surrounding the package and taken out the packing material, all that was left was a silver-colored cloth covering Socrates. She placed the heavy pot carefully on the table. Then, as if she were unveiling a statue, she pulled off the cloth.

Socrates!!

"Oh, my God," whispered Diana.

She fell to her knees.

"Oh, my God!"

All she could do was stare at Socrates, not even able to blink her eyes. Socrates was a rose bush with four black roses. Four black roses!...

Unconscious of time, Diana gazed in wonder at Socrates.

Four black roses!

Diana jumped up and immediately ran to the silver frame her mother had given her as her last birthday gift. After caressing the four black roses ornamenting it, one rose placed on each of the four sides, she read the inscribed verse:

No, it's not what you think.
You have not lost me;
I speak to you through everything,
From behind the remembrances...

As Diana's eyes ran over the words, it was as though she were journeying into the past.

She remembered some of the things Maria wrote in her letters... What Maria had said to Others: "It's not what you think." And the words her mother had said to Maria in her dream: "You have not lost me." What the pink rose told Maria: "Your mother speaks to you through everything..."

Diana remembered the days she'd spent in the rose garden. The image of Artemis and Miriam entwined together in one pot came before her eyes; parts of their dialogue echoed in her ears. She remembered the things Zeynep Hanim had said. Just like the words in Maria's letters, Zeynep Hanim's words, too, seemed to be those of her mother...

Diana remembered the moment she'd seen her mother in Zeynep Hanim's eyes. It was as if she was now looking into Zeynep Hanim's eyes once again. It was as if those sparkling blue eyes weren't Zeynep Hanim's but her mother's...

Diana remembered the times she'd asked her mother for the key to her 'treasure' and how her mother had always replied that she didn't have it. She remembered the stories her mother had told her… She recalled the story Yellow Flower had sent for Maria… And the yellow roses Senhora Alves had put on her mother's grave.

Each line of the framed stanza reminded Diana of one of Maria's letters, and she felt as if with every second she was getting closer to the missing letter.

The first line, "No, it's not what you think," reminded her of Maria's first letter, her objection to Others… "You have not lost me," reminded Diana of Maria's second letter, her mother appearing in a dream, and telling Maria that she hadn't lost her… And with "I speak to you through everything," Diana recalled the third letter, the pink rose telling Maria that her mother spoke to her through everything… So the clue to the fourth letter had to be hidden in the last line.

Diana repeated it over and over again:

"From behind the remembrances… From behind the remembrances…

"Remembrances… Remembrance…"

"Behind…"

She suddenly fell silent and stretched out her hand toward the frame, this precious remembrance of her mother. Taking the frame down from the wall, she turned it over, and looked behind it.

She hadn't been mistaken! In the upper right corner there was a small keyhole. Remembering the advice Yellow Flower had given in Zeynep Hanim's letter, Diana put the frame down on the table, and ran to her room. There, she opened the drawer at the head of her bed. Her searching fingers fumbled among the paper and pens which filled the drawer until, underneath all of these, they felt a little key taped to the bottom of the drawer.

She clasped the key in her palm. *Thank you, Yellow Flower...*

Returning to the living room, she took up the tightly woven crown of white roses that hung from one of Socrates' branches and gently placed it on her head.

She then picked up the silver frame. The key was so small she dropped it while trying to fit it into the lock. But at the second try, she was able to open the frame. In it, there was a silver tablet on which a letter had been engraved in tiny letters. As she took it out, her heart was beating so fast she could almost hear it thump.

She held the silver tablet that shone like a mirror breast-high in front of her. Two words were written at the top of it: "Maria's address:" Right below these words, she saw the reflection of her face on the shining surface of the tablet.

As she repositioned her crown which had slipped slightly backwards, two tears ran slowly down her cheeks. Without wiping them away, she read her mother's words:

My darling Diana, or, as your father used to call you:

"Maria..."

Your father always used to whisper this name in your ear. But after his death, I didn't want to call you Maria until the time when you are ready to understand the part of you that this name stands for.

What I wanted was that you be compelled to leave your home, cross an ocean, and taste the fear of losing your twin, so that no force would ever be able to make you forget this name.

I'm sorry, my beloved child; in order to send you after Maria, I had to say things which weren't entirely true. Unfortunately, my time was running out and didn't allow me to choose another way. I wanted you to set out on your journey to the rose garden as quickly as possible.

Through this journey which could be regarded as a preparation for the October Rains, I wanted you to kill your "self" which causes you such unhappiness and prevents you from following your dreams.

Since this letter is in your hands, you must have made a good start on the path of roses. You must have recognized the difference of the rose garden you've seen.

If that is so... If that garden is indeed different from all other gardens for you, if Socrates is different from all other roses, if the 'you' in that garden is different from all other 'you's... And if this difference, instead of giving you a feeling of superiority, humbles you and gives you the feeling of embracing the whole world, then, my darling, Zeynep and I invite you to Ephesus in October. Since it is only through the October Rains that you can truly know Maria...

Who knows, maybe I'll defy all the laws of physics and come to Ephesus riding on a winged horse so that I can embrace my daughter, so that I can stand with you in the October Rain…

But even if you don't see me there, my darling, listen well to the voices in Ephesus… You'll soon realize that in Ephesus, there's only one voice, not two. Maria's voice… Your voice…

If, one day, that voice should say, "Withdraw all the applications you've made to law firms, place a blank page before you and begin writing the first book of your career," then I have one word of advice for you, darling. In your book, tell us the oldest tale of all:

A journey that begins and ends with you…

By living this tale, you've already written it, now all you have to do is put it down onto the pages.

Perhaps on one of those pages, you may want to use the prized saying that Zeynep promised you in reward for hearing roses. It is from Yunus Emre, a Sufi saint:

"There is one Me within me, deep inside of me."

I love you, my precious one… And I am always with you.

Your mother

Part Three

44

September 19

My Beloved Mother,

The possibility of being reunited with you after so many months fills me with indescribable happiness. In exactly one month's time, I am coming to Ephesus! So that I can stand with my mother in the October Rain…

For the past four months, I have been working on my first novel. I wish I could read my story to you, but unfortunately, it isn't quite ready yet. However, I'd still like to give you the feel of it.

The story is about a rose, Mom. The Rose of Ephesus… A rose that has been created with a divine scent. This scent has a voice of its own. A voice of happiness. It speaks of dreams. It speaks of angels, and it speaks of meeting God in this world.

But as the rose grows, she begins to hear another voice, a voice which she mistakes for her own, a voice which says "me" all the time. It is loud. So loud that the rose can no longer hear her original voice.

The rose needs to take care of her scent in order to hear this voice again. But she is planted in a place where people don't love her for her scent. They are only concerned with her color, her stem and her petals...

So, in the hope of earning their love, she fashions herself into what others want her to be. People say, "grow higher," so she grows higher. People say, "shine up your petals," so she does it in a silent rush. And before long, out of neglect, her scent begins to fade away.

Having shaped her, people shower praises on her as if she were a goddess, and soon the rose starts believing that she is one. She doesn't realize that the only thing she needs to feel special is to recall that she is a rose. Nothing great. Just a rose…

With each passing day, she finds herself becoming more and more unhappy. There remains only one happiness in her life. Her mother. But, at a time she begins to discover her mother, at a time she needs her the most, she loses her forever. Or so she thinks.

Actually, Mom, this story is not about the rose. It is about a mother. It is about a mother who has proven that real roses never die, that they continue to release their perfume even after they fade… It is about a mother who had to shake the pot of the rose so that she could recall…

Will this be possible? Will she recall what she has forgotten, or forget all she has been taught? Will she be able to reclaim her scent? And above all, will she be able to hear her original voice?

I certainly hope so...

Well, Mom, this is more or less the story of my novel. I'm not sure if I was able to tell it properly, though. I feel it's more of a story that one has to live than tell. I couldn't even describe the taste of an olive to Zeynep Hanim, so how could I possibly describe the magic of the rose garden?

But even if I failed, it's okay. It's okay if I couldn't tell it well, it's okay if others don't like it… The story is meaningful to me. Because it is about you. I am glad I told it. Actually no, I didn't. You told it to me. You told it to me at a time when I thought you could never tell me another story.

Thank you, Mom…

I feel your perfume in the air. Each time I breathe it in, it smells different.

Rose scent. Everywhere.

Diana

45

As I am about to finish my novel, I catch sight of blue balloons in bunches of five or six flying past the window. Where can they be coming from?

I open the window to see what is happening. Something is going on in the park. With difficulty, I make out the words written on the large cloth banner:

The Changing Seas of Brazil

Street Art Exhibition

September 24–27

After adding to my novel this chapter in which I see the blue balloons, I leave the house to attend the opening of the exhibition.

46

When I arrive at the exhibition, I see about twenty paintings ranged side by side. My eyes search for Mathias, but I can't see him. I examine the paintings, looking for the one he did while he was here. Just then, I notice my fortuneteller waving at me.

"You're in luck, little lady. See who's here?"

I smile. "Hey, we don't even know why he's here."

"Let's live and see," he says.

"Yes, let's live and see," I say. "Oh, by the way, yesterday, I talked with Senhora Alves. She says 'Hi' to you. But she's still wondering why you didn't accept her gift."

"Why should I accept her gift? I'm a man of honor and I respect my job. If I didn't tell you any fortune, I don't accept any gift or bucks for it."

"Well, maybe you didn't really tell my fortune, but you did get me to start reading those letters somehow. Couldn't you have accepted Senhora Alves' gift as a small token in return for helping her and my mother, a small appreciation for your kindness?"

"Gift in return for kindness, hey? Sounds more like trading to me, little lady. Kindness is ..."

He stops, and points to the other beggars.

"You see the beggars over there? They used to be the luckiest beggars in town, their bellies full from morning till night. You've ever opened your eyes and seen what they ate? We all ate off silver dishes. Every morning, some kid would bring us delicious food, then take off. We all ate for free, long time till the food stopped coming. We all wondered who sent the dishes, but that kid, he too tight-assed to tell! The others, they still don't know to this day, who that goodhearted person was who sent our food. But me, I know because it's been just six months when the food stopped coming. Now you tell me, little lady, who do you think sent all that grand food?"

"I don't know, some kind of charity organization maybe?"

He smiles. "You see, little lady, kindness is that even your daughter doesn't know about the good deed you do."

I don't know what to say. But once again, I feel special to be my mother's daughter.

"I'm sorry, I didn't know. I'll inform the kitchen services as soon as I get back to the hotel, I'll make sure the food will come and—"

"No need," he says. "Just wanted to tell why I turned down that sweet Alves lady's gift. Now don't you worry your pretty head about these, you just go and see the pictures."

"Thanks," I say, patting his back.

Leaving him, I walk toward the group standing ahead of me. They are studying the picture Mathias painted when he was here. When I inspect the painting carefully, I realize that Mathias hasn't come back for me. He'd said he would hold his exhibition where he painted the best picture. And indeed, this painting is really the best of all. The rage of the waves has increased even more and there is still only one seagull in the top corner. Doesn't this bird ever get tired of flying alone?

Suddenly, I notice Mathias. He is standing in the middle of the group with his back turned toward me. Next to him is a man with a price list in his hand. Coming closer, I overhear the man say, "We like this picture the most, especially my wife, if you could reduce the price a bit—"

"That's my favorite one, too," Mathias says. "I'd be more than happy to make a reduction and—"

He stops when he notices I am standing right beside him. Staring at me, he doesn't say a word, not even "Hello." His eyes are fixed on my forehead as though he has just seen the strangest thing in the world.

Fifteen or twenty seconds pass before he turns to the customer again. "But, unfortunately, I can't sell a painting which isn't finished yet."

"If it isn't finished, then why did you include it in the price list?"

"I'm sorry, sir. But I've only realized that just now." He points to the sea. "I painted the sea at exactly this time of day, looking at that exact spot... Look, don't you think there's more light on the face of the water? Somehow I missed seeing how bright it is."

Mathias' eyes keep glancing at me as he apologizes to the man. This seems to annoy the man. Grumbling something in his wife's ear, he takes her by the arm and walks away.

Mathias turns to me. "I don't know what to say, Diana. I'm really—"

"Don't say anything."

"I won't ask you how you are because I see you look exceptionally well. I can't help wondering what's happened since I—"

"Long story," I say. "In fact, one could even write a novel about it."

"I'd love to hear it."

47

After a short walk during which none of his questions are answered, we arrive home.

"Please sit wherever you like. But promise me you won't get up until I'm done. I have to write something for a while."

"Okay, I promise," he says and sits down in the armchair by the window, placing the unfinished painting on his lap.

I hit the key to print the first few pages of my novel. As I continue typing my story, he busies himself with his painting.

Just as I finish writing the part up to where we return home from the park, Mathias puts down his brush and begins to look at me. He has the expression of a happy child. Hmmm, I wonder if I should invite him to Ephesus...

But how would I do that? Especially since I don't even know what we'll be doing in Ephesus. Zeynep Hanim has turned out to be as firm as my mother and Senhora Alves in not revealing a secret. The only thing I know for certain is that I'm going there to get to know Maria better. Now how am I supposed to explain this to Mathias?

Will the little information I have about it make this small town on the other side of the world appeal to him? What is there for Mathias at Ephesus? The ruins of an ancient city... The temple of Artemis... The house of Santa Maria... Will all this be enough to persuade him to come?

Of course, *I* will be there, too! This should be enough to convince him to come.

"I see you've got your nose in the air again," says Maria, interrupting my thought. This happens often now. Whenever the Artemis inside me rears her head, I hear Miriam objecting to her. Sometimes Diana is louder, sometimes Maria... It seems it'll take a while before they become one rose. But I'm glad that now I can at least distinguish between their voices.

So... Would Mathias really come to Ephesus?

And if he did...

Perhaps one October evening, we'd be sitting by the side of the Meles Stream with Mount Bulbul in front of us, watching the sunset.

Perhaps I'd be telling Mathias about the things which took place in Ephesus nearly two thousand years ago. Things I knew from what I've read. Or perhaps after hearing the sounds rising from ancient Ephesus myself.

Maybe, I'd tell him something about the human condition, too. "We are all like the city of Ephesus," I'd say to him, "home to both Artemis and Santa Maria."

And to confuse him even more, I'd also tell him about Artemis' twin brother, Apollo. Then, I'd frown at him and say, "Don't mind Apollo. You, too, search for your missing twin!"

If, on an October evening, everything turns out just the way I imagine, I myself may witness the truth of Zeynep Hanim's words:

"Dreams are the leaven of reality."

48

Just as I begin writing the last chapter, I see Mathias holding out the painting to me. Finished by the addition of one small touch, a third wing shining in between the wings of the lone seagull reveals a second seagull hidden behind it.

I can't take my eyes off the painting, but I continue to write. A few sentences more and then… I'll take the first pages of my novel from the printer and hold them out to Mathias.

Then I'll look into his eyes for a moment, thinking of the two wine bottles in the first chapter... I'll think of the beginning and the end… The two waves in Mathias' little story… Artemis and Miriam… The two seagulls in the painting… Maria and me… And, most important of all, I'll think of Mom and me.

My heart will tell me the very same thing about all of these. So that Mathias, too, may know what my heart says, I'll read out the first words of my novel to him:

"Two are One."

Epilogue

Ephesus! City of duality. Home to both the Temple of Artemis and the holy House of Mother Mary. The city which embodies both the ego and the soul. The epitome of both vanity and humility. The personification of enslavement and freedom. Ephesus! The city in which opposites intertwine. The city that is as human as every living soul.

One October evening, two people were sitting by the side of the Meles Stream near that city—the ancient city of Ephesus. The sun was about to hide itself behind Mount Bulbul, dyed crimson by its rays. Those who understood the language of the skies had brought them the glad tidings of the approaching rain.

"Saint Paul is preaching to the people about Mother Mary," Diana said. "Can you hear the crowd yelling, protesting and cursing him in anger? Thousands are rebelling against the new religion which forbids them to worship their own goddess. Listen to them stamping their feet and shouting, 'We don't want Mary! We worship Artemis!'"

"Artemis?" Mathias asked. "The goddess? The Roman Diana?"

"Don't mind her," Diana said. "She's nothing but an illusion, shaped and worshipped by Others."

"You seem to know a lot about her."

"I know her like I know myself."

"Well then, won't you tell me something about her?"

"She is the goddess of the hunt," Diana began. "A true huntress who uses her arrow to offer a sudden, sweet death to her enemy. Free-spirited yet enslaved, dependent yet proud. Supported by an olive tree, her mother Leto gave birth to her and…"

After taking a deep breath, Diana added, "And to her twin…"

Touching Matthias' hand, "I'll come to her twin, Apollo, later," she said. "I'll tell you about his temple and the most significant words 'Gnoti Seavton' carved on its façade. I'll also tell you about the great philosopher, Socrates, who couldn't take his eyes off these two words when he saw them as he was passing by the temple of Apollo one day. *Gnoti Seavton*, the two words which reveal the reason why the whole universe was created, the reason why we exist. But first, I'd like to tell you about the rose twin of Artemis, the twin that neither Artemis nor Homer knew of.

"According to legend," continued Diana, "one day Artemis learns from her mother that she has a twin of a completely different kind. She leaves home to search for her, crosses an ocean and enters a rose garden where she is asked to offer herself a sudden, sweet death. It is said that she would have to listen to the voice of the roses in order to find her twin.

"After spending some time in the garden, Artemis returns home and finds a key which would lead her to her twin. She's overjoyed to find it, yet her joy is not unclouded. She can't help asking herself, 'Was the art of hearing roses only a myth?' But then she remembers what the gardener had told her on her first day in the garden, and so her heart finds comfort. 'A print placed into your heart,' the gardener had said. 'It may not be apparent now, but when the right time comes, it'll be manifest.'"

Gazing at the rain clouds on the horizon, "Perhaps that time is this time, Jon," added Diana. "Look, the October Rain is approaching..."